"I could rub ___
we go," she s___

"Worker's compensation?" he asked, his eyes sparkling, as if he knew exactly why she'd offered. She'd practically drooled over him when she'd seen him shirtless.

"Just for a little while," he said after a few seconds.

"Shirt off, please," she said, aiming for casualness.

He unbuttoned it, then tossed it onto the second chair. Becca set her hands on his shoulders. His skin felt warm and smooth, his muscles bunched and tight.

"Relax," she said quietly. "It'll be more effective."

She felt his shoulders relax but noticed that he wasn't shutting his eyes, his gaze aimed at the kitchen. To distract himself? Did he think he wouldn't feel her touch as much?

"Close your eyes, Gavin. Enjoy it."

"I might enjoy it too much."

Dear Reader,

How do you measure success? In *Husband for Hire,* I explore that question, seeking answers to a subject that is individual and personal. What constitutes success can only be defined by the individual, obviously, but there are universal aspects, especially regarding the balance of work and play. Now and then we need to slow down, step back and take a look at where we've been, where we are and where we're going. And if we don't like what we see, we need the courage to change.

Change is hard, as my characters Gavin and Becca discover, but well worth the journey. Learning to stop and smell the roses isn't a cliché for them, but a necessary action to peace of mind—and to finding love.

I hope you enjoy their journey.

Susan

HUSBAND
FOR HIRE

SUSAN CROSBY

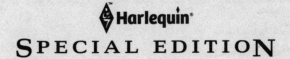

♦ Harlequin®

SPECIAL EDITION

Recycling programs
for this product may
not exist in your area.

ISBN-13: 978-0-373-65600-4

HUSBAND FOR HIRE

Printed in U.S.A.

Books by Susan Crosby

SUSAN CROSBY

believes in the value of setting goals, but also in the magic of making wishes, which often do come true—as long as she works hard enough. Along life's journey she's done a lot of the usual things—married, had children, attended college a little later than the average coed and earned a B.A. in English. Then she dived off the deep end into a full-time writing career, a wish come true.

Susan enjoys writing about people who take a chance on love, sometimes against all odds. She loves warm, strong heroes and good-hearted, self-reliant heroines, and she will always believe in happily-ever-after.

More can be learned about her at www.susancrosby.com.

For Jerry and Linda, a hardworking couple who also remember to stop and smell the roses— and the cactus! You're such an inspiration.

Chapter One

"I knew it," Gavin Callahan said, aiming his fork at his sister Shana. "I knew you had an ulterior motive for inviting me to lunch."

The downtown Sacramento bistro teemed with lunchgoers whose voices echoed in the small space. Gavin had been thoroughly enjoying a well-prepared Cobb salad—until Shana dropped her bombshell.

"Hear me out before you dismiss the idea altogether," Shana said, flicking her golden-blond hair out of her face. "You'd only be pretending to be someone's husband for two days. That's all. Two short days out of your life. Really, Gavin, what else are you doing, anyway? You're on leave from work.

You're single. You're free to come and go. It could be fun."

"It doesn't interest me in the least. And I took a leave of absence for a reason, Shana."

"Please, please, please," she begged. "You won acting awards in high school. You were good! It'll be fun, *and* you'll be doing me a favor that could end up boosting my career with the agency. Pretty please, Gavin. You want to help a single mom struggling to raise a baby girl, don't you? Your own sweet niece…"

Gavin laughed at her dramatic cajoling. At twenty-nine, she was five years younger than he. They hadn't been particularly close while growing up, and until recently they hadn't even seen each other for ten years, although that hadn't been his fault.

"You're aware of what I've been through in the past year," he said. "I was assaulted by enough lies to know I wouldn't want to deliberately participate in one myself. Plus, I respect the institution of marriage. And another thing, how do you think anyone successfully fakes being married, even for two days?" He shook his head. "I'll pass."

Shana reached across the table and grabbed his hand. "I'm serious about this helping my career," she said earnestly. "Julia Swanson—she's the one who owns the temp agency—is desperate. If I can find a man to take the job, she'll think of me first for the really good jobs that come in. The more money I make, the less dependent I am on anyone else. I want to stand on my own, Gavin."

"Now you've stooped to emotional blackmail?" he asked, although his heart did twist just a little.

"Did it work?" She looked hopeful and expectant, with just enough mischievousness in her eyes to make him smile.

He took a sip of water, watching her, letting her wait. Finally he said, "I'll meet with this Julia Swanson and see what she has to say."

Shana bounced up and ran around the table to hug him, almost choking the breath out of him.

"I'm not promising anything," he said sternly.

"Julia can talk anyone into doing anything." She looked smug as she sat down again. "You have a one-o'clock appointment with her, so hurry up and finish your lunch."

"Pretty sure of yourself," he said, catching their server's attention to get the bill.

"'Be prepared,' you know," she quipped. "Her office is on the third floor of the building across the street. I'll go with you."

"You've done enough, thank you. I can take it from here."

She wrinkled her nose at him. "Call me when you've decided, either way, okay?"

"You'll be the first to know." They walked outside. Shana pointed to the building. "Don't get your hopes up," he said, then hugged her, relieved to feel the few pounds she'd put on recently. She was still too slender, but it was progress.

Gavin made his way to the office of At Your Service, a high-end clerical and household staffing business. For the past few months Shana had been working temp jobs through the agency—nicknamed by its clients "Wives for Hire." Or in this case, Gavin thought, "Husband for Hire." He wondered if this spin on their nickname had ever happened before.

"Ms. Swanson will be right with you," a pretty brunette receptionist said to him after he entered the quiet, tasteful office. "Please make yourself comfortable."

Although several chairs were lined up in the reception area, Gavin couldn't sit. Instead he wandered over to a window overlooking the busy street below. He could almost feel the energy—mostly negative—crackling inside him. He didn't like being placed in this position. He wanted Shana to be successful, but—

"Hello, Gavin," said a smooth, female voice from behind him. "I'm Julia Swanson. Please come in."

The woman was ageless and elegant, from her demure ash-blond upsweep to her sage-green suit to her four-inch heels, which brought her within a couple of inches of his six feet. He followed her into her office. On the wall behind her wide, mahogany desk was the company logo, along with the words *When you need the personal touch*...printed in gold-script lettering, classy and subdued, like everything else about Julia Swanson's business.

"Have a seat," she said as she sat behind her desk.

"Thanks," he said, glancing at her window. "I've been living in San Francisco for so long, I forget Sacramento has a distinctive skyline of its own."

"I love this town. It's a big city but with a neighborhood feel." She opened a folder on her desktop. "Your sister wasn't exaggerating."

"Knowing Shana, I'm not sure I want you to explain that."

Julia smiled. "She said you were tall, surfer-blond and handsome."

"Surfer?" He shoved his fingers through his hair, long overdue for a cut. "That's payback for me calling her Goldilocks since she was a kid, I suppose."

"I understand a man in your position would normally never take nor even need to take a temporary job like this," Julia said. "It pays well, but I think that's beside the point for you. Frankly you'd be doing me a favor, and you don't owe me anything."

"On the contrary. Shana has blossomed since she got involved with At Your Service. My sister Dixie and I are grateful. A favor wouldn't be out of order here. Which is why I'm here talking to you, at least."

"Thank you for that. Someone gave me a big break once. I never forget it."

Gavin had also gotten a few breaks here and there.

He remembered how grateful he'd been, had tried to repay the generosity when he could.

"I admire Shana," Julia said. "She's incredibly hardworking but also flexible, which is often an even more important quality in this field. What describes you, Gavin?"

"I've been accused of working 24/7, which is not true. It's more like 18/7. And in my line of work, being flexible is also critical." He shrugged. "You do understand that I'm here only because Shana begged me? The job itself doesn't really interest me, especially the lying. I doubt I could do it."

Julia settled in more comfortably, a small smile on her face. He could usually pinpoint a woman's age, but this woman could be on either side of forty by several years.

"That goes both ways, Gavin. I'm not sure about you yet, either, even with your sister's glowing recommendation. I did find a lot about you online."

He waited for her to follow up on that statement, but she left it there, hanging.

"I take it I passed or I wouldn't have gotten this far in the process," he said.

"The only blemish anywhere in your background was your recent legal problem, but that's resolved, I see. I do require your permission to run a credit check before I recommend you to the client. It speaks to character, you know."

"My 'recent legal problem,'" he repeated, wondering how long it would take before it stopped hurting when he thought about it. "Resolved but not forgotten. And your client has been vetted also? I don't want to worry about her trying to take advantage of my virtuous nature."

Julia laughed softly. "Yes, she's been thoroughly investigated. On paper and in person, she comes across as decent, except…"

He waited through her silence until he couldn't stand it any longer. "Except?"

"I'm trying to find the right word. She's desperate, but I think that's her current state, not her norm. I imagine you're a pretty good judge of character, so why don't you just meet her and see for yourself?"

He found it interesting that Julia called the client desperate. Shana had called Julia that, yet the cool, calm woman gave no hint of desperation. "And if I don't take the job?"

"We've got nine days. I'll fill the position. Maybe not with someone who meets the requirements as well as you do, but that's not your problem, is it?"

Oh, she was good. A velvet steamroller. He saw why she was successful, especially in the high-end market, where charm and good taste mattered a lot.

"All right. I'll talk to her," he said, not promising anything else.

Julia passed him two forms. One gave her permission to run his credit check, the other was already filled out with the name Rebecca Sheridan and an address. "I'll call you on your cell phone to cancel the interview if something in your credit check doesn't cut it. Otherwise, she'll be available at six o'clock at home. I'll let her know to expect you. If you'll call and leave me a message when your interview is over, I'd appreciate it."

"Of course."

They stood and shook hands, their eyes meeting. He wondered what her story was. She didn't wear a wedding ring. No personal photos sat on her desk. Women tended to have pictures visible, especially of their children.

"Thank you, Gavin. Shana deserves a bonus."

"I haven't said yes."

Julia smiled slowly. "Yet."

Gavin said goodbye and left the office, taking the stairs, not willing to wait for the elevator. He emerged into the late-April day breathing normally for what seemed like the first time in…well, in a year, if he was being honest. He had something other than himself to focus on at last.

He could thank his bossy kid sister for that. Maybe, in time, he would.

Becca Sheridan was running late. Like the rest of her coworkers she rarely left work before seven o'clock. Today she had an appointment at six, which meant she had only fifteen minutes to walk to her downtown, high-rise loft and tidy things up a little before the candidate arrived. Gavin, she recalled. Gavin Callahan.

A nice name, she decided. He sounded professional.

Suki Takeda leaned into Becca's open doorway. "Are you excited?"

"I can't believe I'm going along with this ruse."

"It'll get your brothers off your back, won't it?"

"If I can convince them it's true." Becca gave her best friend a doubtful look then grabbed her briefcase. "You know them. They're suspicious by nature."

"If you convince Eric, the other three will buy it." Suki looked around as if she were a spy, her short black ponytail quivering with the quick movements. "You made a good decision to use an agency instead of asking one of the guys here."

"I couldn't take that chance. This way it's a business deal only. No strings. No repercussions."

"Call me when he leaves." Suki pointed a finger at Becca. "If you don't, you can bet I'll show up on your doorstep. I really do think you ought to meet at a coffee shop, you know."

"I know. But the agency checks everyone out. I'll be fine." She hugged Suki as she rushed out her office door. "Wish me luck."

"Luck!"

The cheerful shout stayed with Becca as she was leaving the office, waving goodbye. Craig was tossing a basketball into the air over and over, as usual, doing his best thinking at the same time, according to him. Jacob and Morgan were challenging each other with online search games, part of their job. Chip, the president and CEO, might be in his office or playing Ping-Pong in the company rec room.

No one asked why she was leaving early. Staff came and went at their own hours, for the most part. It only mattered that the work got done and that the only arguments between coworkers were about creative differences.

Becca couldn't remember the last time she'd walked home when the street was this noisy with traffic and crowded with people. What she needed was a moment of calm. Maybe the man would be late and she could catch her breath first....

Although it wouldn't bode well for him if he wasn't on time for their first meeting, she thought.

She rushed into the lobby of her shiny, modern high-rise, then took the stairs to the fourth floor. When she turned the corner of her hallway she saw a man leaning against the wall next to her door, his hands in his pockets.

Her heart skipped a beat. She'd heard the expression for years but hadn't known how it felt. Her heart did skip, then it pounded once, a loud, powerful thump to jump-start itself. He was gorgeous—tall and lean, with streaked blond hair, long enough to curl against his neck.

And green eyes, she noted when she reached him, direct and intelligent. Straight white teeth.

She'd hit the jackpot.

"Gavin Callahan?" she asked, finding her voice.

"Yes. Rebecca Sheridan?" He smiled as he said it,

looking into her eyes as if she were the most beautiful woman he'd ever seen.

"Everyone calls me Becca. I apologize for keeping you waiting," she said, extending her hand, not even startled at the sizzle of electricity when their skin touched. She'd known it would happen.

Just as she knew he was going to be trouble, too.

"I was early," he said, releasing her hand, which continued to tingle.

"Please come in." She unlocked her door and preceded him into the space that was even more disastrous than she'd remembered. "I'm sorry about the mess. I got home around midnight from a week in Chicago." Which accounted for her suitcase and a few other items, but not the piles of magazines, folders and other paperwork that had accumulated on most surfaces.

"I need help, obviously," she said, smiling apologetically. "Can I get you something to drink?"

"Water's fine, thanks."

"I have iced tea, if you'd like." She opened her refrigerator and looked inside. She'd shopped before going to work this morning. "I picked up some cheese and crackers. Will you join me? I'm starving." And stalling. Explaining what she wanted him to do wasn't easy. In fact, it was downright embarrassing.

"Um, sure." He came up to the bar separating the kitchen from the combination dining and living room. The counter was piled with paperwork. Around the room were a lot of moving boxes, taped shut.

"Did you just move in?" he asked.

"Five months ago," she said, unwrapping the cheese plate. "I don't have much spare time. I'm gone more than I'm home, and it's not unusual for me to work twelve-hour days."

"Julia didn't tell me anything about you. What kind of work do you do?" he asked.

"I'm vice president of operations and business development at Umbrella Masters, Inc. It's a computer cloud company."

"I have no idea what that means."

She had to explain what the business was so often, she'd memorized a response, which she recited as she poured two glasses of iced tea. "It's internet-based computing where our customers don't have to own the physical infrastructure but can rent usage from a third-party provider. Through the cloud, as it's called, the customer can use or borrow someone else's network when they need it rather than buy it themselves. It saves the customers time, money and resources in a big way. It's a business still in its infancy, but it's creating serious revenue waves."

"Do you like it?"

"I love it." *I'm just exhausted all the time.* "I'm one of the founders, so the rewards of building something from the bottom up have been huge and satisfying."

"What'd you do on your trip to Chicago?"

She spread some crackers on a plate, setting it

on the counter. "Negotiated a contract with a new vendor."

"Successfully?" He carried the two plates as she took the glasses into the living room to put on the coffee table then sat down on the couch.

"Yes, very successful. Oh! I forgot the grapes." She started to stand.

"I'll get them. If you don't mind?"

"No, that's fine. Thanks. They need to be washed." Although she was hungry enough to eat the whole plate of food, she waited for him.

"How do you celebrate a success like that?" he asked from the kitchen, the water running, his voice suddenly seeming far away.

"Maybe with a vacation." She nestled into the cushions a little and yawned. If she could only close her eyes for just a minute. Just a minute.… "I haven't gone anywhere in years because we were building the business. I've been dreaming about Hawaii.…"

Gavin carried the grapes into the living room then noticed her eyes were closed.

He set down the plate. When she didn't budge, he inched closer. Asleep. She had to be completely worn-out to fall asleep in front of a stranger. He'd been that tired many times in his life. Too many. He resisted the temptation to move her shiny brown hair away from her face, where it had fallen.

Now what?

He carried the plate to the kitchen counter, moved some of her papers to the floor and then snacked a little, feeling like an intruder. After a while he put the remainder in the refrigerator. His hands shoved into his pockets, he looked for a way to pass the time, but for all the stacks of reading material, everything seemed to be about business and computers, subjects that generally started him yawning.

He took out his cell phone and played Flight Control for a while but found he was too distracted by her to concentrate. She'd tucked her arms close to her slender body, as if chilled. He wondered if she needed a blanket over her.

Keeping an eye and ear open, he peeked hesitantly into the first doorway and discovered a bedroom, but it was crammed with boxes. The second door led to the master bedroom, which wasn't messy at all but lacked furniture. Without unmaking her bed, he didn't see a blanket, not even a decorative throw. He could go on a hunt, he supposed, but figured she wouldn't appreciate that.

Framed photographs drew him closer to her dresser. The largest frame held a picture of a couple in their wedding finery from years ago—her parents? There was a small candid shot of a maybe five-year-old Becca with the woman from the wedding photo, both wearing matching dresses. There was a newer shot of Becca seated in a red Ferrari convertible, waving both hands high in the air. Hers? Unlikely, given the cost of the car. Several other photos caught his eye, but he didn't take the time to look too closely, not wanting to get caught prying.

From all appearances, she seemed to be a successful woman accustomed to life's comforts, including a loving family. So, why the lie? Obviously she was exhausted, frazzled and disorganized—not endearing traits, at least for him. He liked women who had their act together.

And women who were honest.

She lived on easy street, and now she wanted someone to help her out of a jam she'd gotten herself into. By lying.

He wished he could just leave, but he waited her out. In the end, he needn't have worried about getting caught peeking. She slept for more than an hour, until the colorful sunset sky was framed by her floor-to-ceiling living-room windows, the view tempting enough to lure him onto the outdoor balcony.

But just then her eyes snapped open. She shoved herself upright, her dark brown gaze homing in on him, looking confused.

"Hungry?" he asked, not waiting for her answer, knowing she was embarrassed. He brought the plate to the coffee table. "I already ate," he said, setting down an iced tea, as well.

He watched her stare at the food, saw the flush in her cheeks fade as her discomfort eased, then he told her the decision he'd made while she slept.

"I can't take the job. Good luck to you."

He went straight to the door.

Chapter Two

"**W**ait! Please wait." Feeling gut punched, Becca jumped up to stop him. They hadn't even had a conversation about the particulars of the job itself, and he was turning it down?

"We haven't talked yet," she said.

"I know enough. I can see why you think you need a personal assistant or something," he said. "But that's not why you went to At Your Service, is it? I can't play the part of a doting husband when I'm not. I'm sorry."

The speed of his departure caught her off guard, as well as his judgmental tone. "You're here. You could at least hear me out."

After a moment, he said, "You're right. I should

hear you out. It won't make me change my mind, Becca, but the floor's yours."

He sat at one end of the sofa like a sculpture of the world's most perfect male, his arm stretched along the back, ankle crossed over one knee.

She should be figuring out what to say to him to change his mind, but instead she wondered how bad her hair looked. She'd had it cut to chin length recently, a style she thought would save her time, but which had ended up taking extra minutes to fix every morning.

Needing to pull herself together before saying anything more, she said, "Would you mind waiting a few minutes?"

A few beats passed, then he nodded, although he looked as if he wanted to sigh.

Becca shut the master-bedroom door behind her and leaned against it. He wasn't going to take the job. He was perfect, but he wouldn't be hers, not even for two days.

Unless she could change his mind. She'd been called tenacious but also sincere all her life. It was usually a winning combination. What did she have to lose?

She shoved her hair back from her face and headed into her bathroom then returned to the living room a few of minutes later with her armor on—her hair brushed and fresh lipstick applied. She'd seen in the mirror how tired she looked, so she tried to smile now, knowing that would help.

She also carried a picture frame. She sat next to Gavin and turned the photo around.

"These are my brothers," she said. "Eric, Sam, Trent and Jeff. Eric is oldest. He's thirty-nine, and I'm the youngest. I'm thirty." She set the frame on the coffee table facing Gavin. "They're coming to Sacramento on the Saturday after next to celebrate my wedding."

"Which you didn't have."

"That's true. But they need to think I did."

"Why?"

"Because Eric—" she pointed to him in the photograph "—won't get married until I do. Actually I think it's possible that all four of them are waiting for me to marry first."

"That's ridiculous."

"I know it seems so, and certainly Eric has never confirmed it as fact, but he loves kids and he wants to be married. I know he does."

"Why would his getting married have anything at all to do with you?"

"Because he won't give up feeling responsible for me until he's satisfied I'm being taken care of by a husband."

"You do realize how archaic that sounds, don't you?"

"Of course. But our circumstances are unusual. You see, our parents died when I was thirteen. My brothers took over raising me. It was a group project, but Eric was the patriarch and he always had the last word." She traced a finger across the glass. "They love me. I've never doubted it for a second."

"But?"

"But they also smothered me with that love, Eric most of all. He's been by far the most overprotective. I know there are worse things in life to complain about. I'm lucky in so many ways."

"Do they live close?" he asked.

"No. In fact they're scattered around the country, but they remain in solidarity when it comes to me. It kills them that I'm living alone in a big city.

"And now that I've turned thirty, their desire to get me married and settled has intensified. Are your parents like that?"

"I'm pretty sure it doesn't matter to them. Although maybe my father would like the Callahan name to continue."

"How old are you?" she asked.

"Thirty-four. And nowhere close to marriage. What do you think is behind Eric's need to see you settled down?"

"This is purely speculation on my part, but it's almost as if his job won't be done until then."

"So you're feeling pressure to marry because you want him to do the same?"

"Not just him, but all my brothers, I think. I owe them a lot, Gavin, a whole lot, but Eric most of all. He was twenty-two when our parents died. He'd just graduated from college and would've been off to new places and adventures. Instead he stayed and took care of us. We all went to college. He made sure of that. We're all successful."

"Professionally," Gavin said.

"Meaning?"

"Well, none of you have married, yet you're all in your thirties. Seems that out of five siblings, at least one would've taken the plunge."

Her back stiffened. "Now you see my dilemma. Besides, that's an odd statement from someone who's thirty-four and happily declares he's nowhere close to marriage himself. Don't you consider yourself successful?"

"I'm not the one looking for a pretend spouse."

He had a point. She stacked some cheese and crackers, giving herself something to do with her hands. "Well, I can't speak for my brothers, but I feel not only professionally successful, but personally, as well. I've been happy with my life. For the most part."

She saw him look around her loft, as if reminding her how scattered her life had become. Now, she never invited anyone to visit other than Suki, yet at one time years ago, her home had been party-central.

"So, what are you looking for in a one-weekend husband?" he asked.

"Attentiveness," she answered hopefully.

He laughed.

She smiled. "Seriously, I do have a plan. My brothers are flying in on Saturday morning and leaving Sunday afternoon. Your job would be to convince them we're really married, that you're the real deal, you know? A man who loves me. So, what I need is an actor, although this play is live-action. You need to be able to improvise in a believable way."

He eyed her thoughtfully. "Why did you choose that particular course of action?"

Becca tucked her feet under her, facing him. She had to be honest or the situation wouldn't work. He needed to know everything—even though she was going to look foolish. She could only hope he would take pity on her.

"My brothers have an annoying habit of setting me up with blind dates, a situation that has intensified in the past couple of years. How they come up with these guys is a mystery, especially long distance, but one brother or another sets me up every few months. Every one of these guys is an extreme Alpha male, by the way, just like my brothers. I finally made up a boyfriend. A doctor," she added, trying not to seem too embarrassed by her actions. "I knew he would need to be very successful in order to be found satisfactory. Then they started planning visits here to meet my boyfriend, so I pretended he was part of the Doctors Without Borders organization and sent him out of the country."

Gavin looked surprisingly amused. "It's hard to imagine being able to pull that off for any length of time."

"I know. I didn't think it through. I can be…

impulsive." Which didn't describe her logical and methodical business persona, but did describe her in many other ways. "Eric didn't buy it. After a couple of trips to see me and meet the mysterious boyfriend who was always out of the country, he called my bluff."

She took a sip of her now watered-down iced tea. "My friend Suki and I were out to dinner when Eric called to set me up with yet another blind date. It was the same old argument, with me saying I already had a boyfriend and Eric saying he didn't believe it. Suki said, 'Tell him you eloped.' So I did."

Gavin still looked amused, so she relaxed a little.

"Which Eric also didn't buy," Gavin said. "Because as close as you are, he knows you wouldn't leave him out of your wedding plans."

She nodded. The hurt in Eric's voice still haunted her. "I told him that my husband had been about to leave on a particularly dangerous assignment, and we wanted to marry before he went. I can't tell you how much I regretted the lie—*still* regret it. But in the end it served two important purposes. It got my brothers off my back about getting married, which I will do in my own way and time, and it opened the door for them to stop worrying about me and move on with their own lives."

"I still find it hard to believe they haven't married because you haven't."

"I know it seems like I'm reaching, but you don't

understand what happens when you lose both your parents at the same time, especially at such young ages. It created an unusual bond between us as siblings."

"And yet you don't feel you can be honest with them."

"I get that you probably think I'm crazy—or worse. Certainly I could've set things right since I made up the marriage. I could even pretend to get a quick annulment, but that would give my brothers free rein to start in again, and wouldn't accomplish what I want most of all—for them to put themselves first for once, especially Eric."

Gavin picked up her iced-tea glass and headed into the kitchen. What was he thinking? Had she been too honest? Did she seem pathetic?

He returned in a minute with a fresh glass, ice cubes clinking, and handed it to her. He must have needed a moment to take it all in.

This made her hopeful. Except he didn't sit down again.

"I admit I don't understand your connection with your brothers," he said. "My family life didn't and doesn't resemble yours in the least. I don't identify with your bond, not to the point of creating such a lie. And even though it sounds somewhat intriguing, you need to find someone else. I'm sorry. Good luck, Becca. Goodbye."

He walked out, pulling the door shut quietly behind him. The moment it closed she felt as if she were drowning in a silent pool of disappointment and, well, shame. His saying it all out loud *did* make her seem pathetic. Maybe no one else could ever understand the obligation she felt to her brothers, especially Eric.

Becca let out the breath she'd been holding. She picked at the food but had lost her appetite, so she cleaned up the dishes then carried her suitcase into her bedroom to unpack. Her eyes stung. She sat on the bed and tried not to cry.

What a mess she'd created for herself.

Gavin took the elevator to the basement-level parking and headed for the visitor parking. He couldn't believe he'd even entertained the idea of taking the job—even for Shana. What had he been thinking?

And yet…he was intrigued. Maybe because he'd watched her sleep, as vulnerable as a child. She'd lost the mother in the photo with the matching dress. She'd been left with domineering brothers who obviously adored her, even if they didn't acknowledge her as an independent adult.

But was that any reason to lie? Couldn't she just stand up for herself?

He reached his car but didn't unlock it. She'd also wanted a doctor. He laughed a little, the sound echoing in the concrete structure. He hadn't bothered to tell her he was a doctor—one on a break for who knew how long. He wasn't even sure he wanted to continue in medicine, not after what he'd been through.

If he did the job for her he would have to take down his Facebook page....

Dammit. Why couldn't he just let it go?

He knew the answer. Because spending time with a scattered woman could be a good distraction right now while he made some life decisions.

Or, more likely, drive him crazy.

He climbed into his car, slid the key in the ignition. Really, why should he do it?

First, he recognized a workaholic when he saw one. He'd driven himself too hard, too, for reasons he'd never stopped to analyze beyond the usual escape-from-a-small-claustrophobic-town need that many young people feel after high school when the future is a blank canvas.

He certainly hadn't experienced the deep family ties she had, but he understood how important they were to her.

Second, he liked her. More than that—he was attracted to her, which could be problematic in the long run.

Third, as Shana had reminded him, he had no life at the moment.

Fourth, and maybe most important, he needed to feel needed.

After a minute, he started the engine, his mind made up. All the reasons he'd listed were self-serving. They were about him, not her.

And it really should be about her.

Just as abruptly, he turned off the ignition. He'd left with barely a goodbye, bordering on rudeness, which wasn't like him. For her sake he would go back and talk to her, explain why he was the wrong person, tell her the kind of person she should be looking for instead. One who wouldn't be in it for his own selfish purposes.

He owed her that much, and Shana and Julia, too. He didn't want to give the agency a bad rap.

Right. That was why he was going back upstairs to see Becca Sheridan.

Becca was back at square one, and she really didn't want to go through the process of explaining herself again, especially since telling him the story had let her see how truly pitiable it was.

Aside from that, Gavin had intrigued her, especially his integrity. She was offering a lot of money for a day and a half's work, and he hadn't jumped at it, which said something. He wouldn't take the job just for the money.

She had to take his lead and tell the truth. It was too late to call Eric tonight, but first thing in the morning—

Her doorbell rang.

Suki. She'd forgotten to call her. And now she'd find Becca looking red and puffy after a good, long crying jag. Becca didn't want to talk, not even to her best friend in the world, but she figured Suki might call the police if she didn't get an answer, worried that the "candidate" had harmed her in some way.

She opened the door.

It wasn't Suki, but Gavin, looking determined. Then his eyes narrowed.

"Have you been crying?"

Hope got mixed up with embarrassment once again. Why did he keep catching her when she looked her worst? "Do I really need to answer that?"

After several seconds of just staring at her, his expression changed. He looked…resigned.

"Tell me if I've summed this up correctly," he said. "You lied about having a boyfriend for *your* sake—to get them off your backs about it. But you lied about having a husband for *their* sakes—to let them to move on with their lives and futures."

He put her reasoning into words much better than she had. "Yes, exactly."

"Then, okay, I'll do it. I understand wanting your siblings, especially Eric, to be happy. I get that they've given up a lot for you," he said. "But I've got a few requirements of my own."

Relief and joy battled inside her. "Come in."

He did, but he didn't sit. "Obviously I can't just show up here next Saturday and pretend to be your husband and expect your brothers to buy it. That means we have nine days to become believable. And nine days to get all this—" he gestured around her messy space "—in order. I'm volunteering to do that for you. If you want your brothers to think your life is in good hands, this place needs to reflect that—because it also reflects on me."

She didn't know how she felt about his take-charge attitude, but she knew he was right. "I guess I do need a keeper."

"And I've never been anyone's keeper, but I do need a challenge right now."

"So you would be free all week to help me? I'm not taking you away from another job?"

"I'm between jobs at the moment."

Which could mean anything, she thought. He could have been fired, laid off, or quit. Maybe temp jobs were his mainstay. "What kind of work did you do?"

"My last job was at a hospital."

"Really?" This was even better than she'd hoped. "So you'll be able to toss in a few medical words and sound like you know what you're doing? You could sound like a doctor?"

"As long as no one needs brain surgery."

"When can you start?" she asked, grinning.

"What time do you leave for work?"

"Seven-thirty."

"I'll be here at seven. I'll bring breakfast."

"I don't eat—"

"I'll bring breakfast. I saw the inside of your refrigerator. You have very little on hand." He headed to the door, grabbed the knob. "I have to be home for the weekend, but I'll do an assessment of what needs to be done tomorrow then come back on Monday. I'll call Julia and let her know."

"Wait!" She walked to him, the door open. "How can I reach you?"

"I'll give you my cell-phone number tomorrow. Sleep well." He laid a hand on her shoulder. "Everything will work out, Becca."

With those softly spoken, comforting words, he left.

Becca closed her mouth after a moment, her eyes watering and throat burning. Then she shut the door and went to bed, where she fell asleep within a minute.

Life was good.

Chapter Three

"I'm trying to remember the last time I ate oatmeal," Becca said, scraping her bowl clean. "And I'm sure it didn't taste this good."

Gavin had guessed what she might like to eat and decided on oatmeal loaded with raisins, walnuts and brown sugar for both of them, something hearty he'd picked up at the restaurant of the hotel where he'd stayed overnight.

She looked fresh, her eyes bright, her spirits high. Maybe a little too high. There was nothing leisurely about her this morning. She moved quickly, spoke with rapid-fire speed and continually bounced a foot while talking. He hadn't noticed anything like it last night, but she was definitely wound up now.

"Are you all right?" He picked up her empty bowl and set it in the kitchen sink with his.

She hopped off the barstool. "I feel good. Hopeful."

Hopeful. An interesting word. "What's your plan for your second bedroom? Office? Guest room?"

"Both. Suki has crashed on my couch a few times, but it would be good to have a real guest room."

"How much work do you do at home?"

She scooped up her briefcase, which she'd tossed onto the couch, and checked the contents. "Lots. But I usually sit here on the sofa with my laptop. I don't have to spread out much."

He found himself staring at her rear, which was round and taut, her jeans fitting her like a second skin. She was slender but toned, her breasts small and firm. "Do you need all the trade journals that are stacked up around the place?"

"Probably not." She straightened and faced him in time to find him staring.

He felt like a teenager, caught ogling. It'd been way too long since he'd been on a date, having no interest while the lawsuit was being investigated then tried. He supposed it was a sign of emotional progress that he was thinking about sex again, but it was disconcerting in this situation. For all intents and purposes, she was his boss.

Not to mention she lived in Sacramento and he in San Francisco, too far apart to see each other often. Although in a week's time they would *need* to look as if they were married, with all the intimacy that implied. Interesting contradictions, he thought.

"This is my cell-phone number," he said, passing her a scrap of paper.

"And here's a key for you," she said. "So, I won't see you again until Monday?"

"Right." He could have changed his plans at home but decided he'd rather work without her around— which meant putting it off until Monday. It had been a year since he'd spent time with a woman he liked *and* was attracted to. "You must have a casual workplace," he said, "to wear jeans as a vice president."

She flashed a grin. "Actually I'm dressed up." She pulled an orange cardigan over her crisp white shirt. "We don't see many visitors, although we're doing a lot more video conferencing these days, so some of the guys may need to start wearing dress shirts instead of T-shirts."

Gavin got caught by her smile, which spread from her mouth to her eyes, their dark brown depths sparkling. How she could look both at ease and wound up was beyond him, but it described her.

"If there's something you need me to do over the weekend, let me know," she said as she headed to the door.

"Will you go grocery shopping?"

She frowned. "What for?"

He laughed. "Eat out a lot, do you?"

"I don't have time to cook. Or the interest."

"Then I'll take care of it before I get here on

Monday. I think if you want your brothers to believe you're married, your kitchen should be a little better stocked."

"They know I don't cook."

"People have a different expectation for a married person, I think. I won't overdo it."

She smiled, obviously happy. "We already feel so domestic," she said. "I feel like I should kiss you goodbye and call you honey."

Feel free. The words stayed trapped in his head.

"But I'll just say thank-you. You don't know how relieved I am, Gavin."

"Have a good day. Honey."

She laughed then waved goodbye.

The apartment seemed unbearably quiet after the door shut. Becca Sheridan had presence. He wondered if she knew what a potent force she was.

Gavin planned to spend the next few hours looking through boxes, sorting stacks and making lists. He was excited to get started, anxious to create order out of her chaos. He had work to do, physical and mental.

And he felt better than he had in a long time, lighter, unburdened. Focused.

Sane.

He hoped it was worth living the lie.

Suki shadowed Becca from the front door all the way to her office. She'd been lying in wait, had texted Becca four times this morning demanding to know how the interview had gone. Becca couldn't explain it adequately via text message, so she waited, although knowing Suki would pounce.

"Tall, blond and handsome, like he'd just come out of the ocean with a surfboard under his arm," Becca said as soon as Suki shut the door. "Intelligent. Easygoing. Good manners. Knows how to take care of a person. Jackpot."

She started to laugh after that, feeling like a teenager, light and carefree.

"Wow," Suki said, sitting back in her chair. "And he works as a temp? Something's gotta be wrong with him."

"I kept looking for flaws. I didn't see any."

"Did you make him strip down? Maybe it's where you can't see it."

Becca grinned. "Why didn't I think of that? I could've brought out my casting couch. I'm telling you, he's one gorgeous man. And he intends to take care of my needs."

"Do you have to pay more for that?" Suki waggled her eyebrows.

Warmth suffused Becca. She hadn't intended to give things a sexual spin, but those visions simmered below the surface without conscious thought. She was more than a little attracted to Gavin. If she'd put together the man of her dreams, feature by feature, Gavin Callahan would've been the end result.

"I meant," Becca said to Suki, "that he accepted

the job, and I'm sure he'll do a great job of being a pretend husband."

"Can I have him when you're done?"

Becca had no glib comment in return. She didn't want to share him. *He's mine,* she wanted to say. Then her phone rang, saving her as Suki slipped out of the room and the workday began.

Except it wasn't work related.

"Hey, Bec," her brother Eric said, his voice deep and sure.

Becca always felt safe when she heard him. He'd been her lifeline after she left home, even as she'd craved the independence. "How's life in the Big Apple?" she asked.

"Dog-eat-dog. How's everything with you?"

"Busy and good. I'm looking forward to seeing you. All four of you. Are your plans all set?"

"Our flights will arrive within an hour of each other. Sam and I will hook up in Chicago then fly to Sacramento together. Trent and Jeff will do the same in Dallas. So, only two flights to contend with in the end. We should get to your place around noon."

"I'll have lunch ready." Or catered or something, she thought.

"Are you cooking these days? Have you become the little wife?"

She didn't know why that stung, but it did. "Chauvinist. I think I can manage sandwiches."

"Sounds good. We'll take the newlyweds out to dinner Saturday night, though."

"Thank you. I'll let Gavin make reservations for us all."

"Oh, he has a name finally."

She'd referred to her mystery boyfriend as Doc whenever she spoke of him to her brothers. It had become a joke, although she knew they were annoyed at not knowing the real name of her fantasy man.

"And his last name?" Eric prompted.

"I'm not telling. You can meet him and form your own opinion, not whatever information you might dig up on him in the meantime."

"Spoilsport. And you'll share pictures from your wedding with us, too, since we haven't received any either by mail or email."

A statement, not a question, she realized. "Of course."

There was a moment of silence. Then Eric spoke again. "Are you happy, Bec?"

"I am." Except for lying and deceiving and being attracted to a man without any potential for a future relationship. "Don't be too hard on Gavin, okay? Eloping was my idea."

"He went along with it."

She heard condemnation in his voice. "He'd do anything for me, Eric. Isn't that what you've always wanted?"

He sighed. "Of course it is."

"Then just be happy for me."

She hung up the phone a minute later feeling lower

than low. What a sincerely stupid thing she'd done, even if for what she thought were the right reasons.

After a minute of remorse, she sat up tall in her chair. She would get through the weekend and the lie somehow, because it mattered. She'd made her decision for good reasons, solid reasons. She couldn't backpedal.

Except…now she had another tricky situation to deal with. She drummed her fingers on her desk, debating, and then finally called Gavin's cell phone.

"We have a new complication," she said.

"The first of many, I imagine," he said drily. "What's up?"

"I just talked to Eric. He's looking forward to seeing pictures of our wedding."

There was a long moment of pause. "Okay. You find the right dress to wear. I'll take care of everything else. I'll pick you up around noon on Sunday."

For a woman used to making decisions herself, she gave in easily to his taking charge. "Thank you, Gavin. Thank you so much."

"It's something any good husband would do."

She heard the smile in his voice. "What about your weekend plans?"

"I can be done by then. See you on Sunday."

"Gavin," she said in a hurry before he hung up— and before she lost her nerve.

"What?"

"If your plans include getting a haircut, please don't." She wanted to run her fingers through it, had been hoping for a chance while they were "married."

She could almost hear him frown.

"I should look my best for our wedding photos," he said. "They last a lifetime, you know."

"I think it adds to your philanthropic, selfless-doctor look," she said.

He laughed, soft and low, a sound that registered in her as if their bodies had been touching. She liked him too much. Way too much.

"I guess I can make that sacrifice for my wife."

"Thank you," she said, the phrase becoming all too common. "If there's something you think of that I can do, you'll let me know, right?"

"Look like a bride. I'll handle the rest. And relax, okay? It'll be fine."

"Giving up control is hard for me," she admitted.

"No kidding. Let go of the wheel, Becca. Control's an illusion, anyway, so you might as well just have fun."

Was that his philosophy? Was that why he was happy working temp jobs, not having a particular career? She wished she could be more like him. Well, a *little* more like him. She couldn't give up the career she'd worked so hard for.

"You win," she said. "Please keep track of your expenses."

"See you later." Then he hung up, without waiting for her to even say goodbye.

Becca looked around her office. If she had a window, she would've taken advantage of it to stare outside while she considered their conversation.

Look like a bride, he'd said. She took a mental tour of her closet, but nothing appropriate came to mind. She needed to shop. Normally she would ask Suki to go with her, but she didn't want to involve anyone else, if possible. As it was, Eric would wonder why Suki hadn't attended her best friend's wedding.

A wedding without a honeymoon.

Somehow that didn't seem quite fair.

She laughed, let herself relax as Gavin had pretty much ordered her to and then got down to work. After all, someone had to bring home the bacon in this marriage.

Chapter Four

"How did you find this place?" Becca asked as they pulled into a Lake Tahoe–area parking lot Sunday afternoon after a two-hour drive.

"On the internet," Gavin answered, grateful that the outside of the Hearts Entwined Wedding Chapel matched the picture on the web. It was the newest chapel in the region, so he hoped it would be the nicest—and that the owners were discreet.

"So, they're letting us just take pictures?" she asked. "How did you manage that?"

"Money always talks. For a couple hundred dollars I bought the ceremony, minus the legalities. Not expensive at all." He turned off the ignition and faced her. She looked stunning in her off-white silk suit with the above-the-knee skirt and super-high heels, a fascinating contrast of sweet and sexy.

"I'll reimburse you, of course." She reached over and combed his hair with her fingers, startling him with the action. "There." She let her hand drift away, but her gaze stayed locked with his. "You look very groomlike in your dark suit and white shirt. Very handsome."

The moment turned too serious, or maybe too tense. It was hard to tell. To change the mood he reached into the backseat and pulled out a box. "Your bouquet."

"For me?" Her eyes lit up, and her cheeks turned pink.

He'd genuinely surprised her, which made him happy he'd taken the time to do things right.

"Oh! It's gorgeous!" She pressed her face into the pink-and-white rose bouquet and inhaled the fragrance. "You thought of everything. Thank you!"

Her happiness pleased him like nothing else had in so long. Because she was tempting enough to kiss, he had her pin a white-rose boutonniere on his lapel, her look of concentration making him smile.

When she was done she patted his chest then pulled back in a hurry, as if she'd overstepped.

"We need to look married," he said, capturing her hands in his. "That means touching."

"In front of other people, maybe. Not when it's just us."

"We need to get used to it so it's normal for us,

don't you think?" He acknowledged it was just an excuse to touch her, but it still made sense for their purposes.

"You're very sensible, Gavin."

No, I'm actually all stirred up. He wondered what she would say to that. "Ready?" he asked.

She looked at the building and took a deep breath. "Ready."

He held her hand as they went inside, the interior dark, with rich wood walls and silk-upholstered guest chairs. A floor-to-ceiling oil painting of Lake Tahoe and the Sierra Nevadas held center stage, a beautiful backdrop for photographs to be taken during and after the ceremony.

"Mr. Callahan?" A slight man with white hair approached. "I'm Reverend Sorbo."

"Thank you for fitting us in, Reverend. This is Ms. Sheridan."

The man nodded. "Everything is ready for you. Please follow me."

For the first photos, Gavin and Becca were posed as if reciting their vows, with the reverend in the background between them, then he said, "Rings?"

Becca shot a look at Gavin. "Oh, we don't—"

"Of course we do," he said, interrupting her. He dipped into his pocket and pulled out matching bands, each carved with swirls and dotted with diamond chips.

Her hand shook as he put her ring on her finger, the photographer coming up closer to capture the moment. Gavin found he was a little shaky, as well, and chalked it up to perpetuating the lie. Sometimes he was able to set all that aside, but putting a wedding ring on her brought it to the forefront. Marriage was supposed to be revered and respected.

"Next would be a kiss," Reverend Sorbo said.

Gavin took her hands. Her eyes were so dark they seemed black. He leaned toward her, touched his lips to hers and felt them quiver. He heard the photographer take a couple of shots, then Gavin pulled back.

"You can do better than that, young man," the reverend said with a chuckle. "A picture's worth a thousand words, you know."

"Are you game?" he whispered to Becca.

She nodded. He moved in closer. Then he bent her over his arm and held that pose for the camera. Startled, she looked surprised, then she laughed. Only then did he kiss her, kissing the smile off her face, savoring the taste of her, especially when she started kissing him back making that soft little moan....

Becca forgot everything but him, the way his lips felt, the comfort of his arms holding her securely, even the scent of the light cologne he wore.

Best...kisser...ever. The thought registered in her brain gradually, just as her need for him did, which didn't slam into her but coiled slowly, attaching her to him with heat and desire—until he straightened, taking her with him. He kept his hands curved around her arms, waiting for her to stop wobbling before he released her.

"Much better," the reverend said.

Becca and Gavin stood in front of the grand painting for an official wedding portrait, then they were handed a CD of their photos and sent on their way. In the car they simply sat for a few moments.

"I'll get prints made," Gavin said after a while.

"Okay." She felt married. She shouldn't, since they'd only hit the highlights of a normal ceremony, and they didn't have a license. The usual steps of courtship, marriage proposal and real ceremony hadn't happened, either....

Yet she *felt* married.

She sneaked a look at the ring on her finger.

"They're on loan," he said, starting the engine of the low, sleek sports car he seemed too comfortable with for it to be a rental. Another surprise.

"The rings are gorgeous." Since he'd caught her looking, she held out her hand to better admire the band. "You really did think of everything."

"Can I let you in on a secret?" he asked, smiling and angling toward her.

"I'm good at keeping secrets."

"I found a wedding site online and followed their checklist."

She found that incredibly sweet. Tempted to lay her hand along his hair and kiss him, she just smiled instead.

"Are you hungry?" he asked.

"My appetite has returned." On cue, her stomach growled. She pressed a hand to it and laughed.

"We're a little overdressed for the casinos." He pulled out of the parking lot and headed south.

"Does anyone care about such things? We might stand out a bit, but I wouldn't mind grabbing a bite to eat then feeding a slot machine. I feel lucky today."

They left their wedding flowers in the car, but even the restaurant hostess seemed to recognize them as newlyweds and gave them a quiet corner booth. She took their drink orders before giving them a wink and walking away.

Becca wondered if she should stake Gavin some cash. Julia would've told him what his wages would be for the following weekend, but he'd also spent funds Becca needed, and wanted, to reimburse.

This was different, however. This would be a cash transaction.

Their server placed glasses of iced tea in front of them, and then took their orders for minestrone soup and BLT sandwiches.

"Do you gamble?" Becca asked Gavin when they were alone again.

"Rarely. I'll be happy to stay with you while you play. Unless you'd rather be alone?"

"That would look strange, wouldn't it, since we're supposed to be newlyweds?" She sipped her tea. "So, I think I'll set a limit of fifty dollars to lose."

"Do you always lose?"

"I've only played a few times, mostly during bachelorette parties. I can't remember ever going home with more than I had. How about you?"

"I tend to win, mostly," he said with a shrug. "But I play blackjack not slots."

Becca ran a finger along the drops of condensation on her glass. They'd talked about their childhoods on the drive up earlier, but she realized she'd talked a lot more than he had. Had that been a planned maneuver on his part?

"You said that you had sisters, Gavin. Older or younger?"

He pulled out his cell phone and brought up a photo with two women and a baby. "Dixie's three years younger than me and Shana is five years younger. Dix recently got married. She and her husband are on their honeymoon."

"And Shana?"

"She gets a lot of jobs through At Your Service. That's her daughter, Emma, who's about nine months old now."

"Were you close as children?"

He tucked his phone back in his pocket. "Dix and I were when we were really young. Shana always marched to her own drummer. But all three of us had a kind of bond because our parents didn't really parent. As siblings, we looked out for each other, and yet I can't say we were close. Not like you and your brothers."

"Your parents just let you raise yourselves?" She

couldn't imagine that. Hers had always been there for her—then her brothers had followed suit.

"Sort of. On one hand, they were extremely strict. They set down rules and expected us to follow them, but then they left us alone. If we got caught doing something we shouldn't be doing, the punishment was swift and harsh. I learned not to get caught."

Their lunch was served, the aroma enticing.

"I always got caught," she said with a sigh. "Always. If my parents didn't catch me, one of my brothers did. The freedom when I went away to college was heady. I stayed up too late, waited until the day before a paper was due before I wrote it and partied a lot. But by my sophomore year I'd seen the value in moderation. To a degree, anyway." She grinned. She had loved the college environment. "Did you go to college?"

"Yes. But I was a nose-to-the-grindstone student. Plus I was always working. Between jobs, scholarships and grants, I graduated debt free."

"That's a big accomplishment. What's your degree in?"

"Biology, with a minor in biochemistry."

"That's a tough curriculum."

He shrugged. Gavin steered the conversation to how good the food was, but Becca recognized a diversion when she heard one.

"You said you worked in a hospital before this. What did you do?"

He had taken a bite of sandwich, so he didn't

answer right away. "Whatever needed doing. You could find me in the lab or radiology or even the O.R."

An answer but not an answer, she noticed. "Are you looking for work now?"

"No."

"Why not?"

"I needed a break."

Short answers, no eye contact. He didn't want to talk about it. She ate in silence for a while, and then couldn't stand it any longer.

"Why are you working for At Your Service?" she asked as they finished up.

"As I told you, I'm between jobs, and my sister knew it. When this position came up, she thought I'd get a kick out of it. I did some acting in high school. She thought that qualified me."

"Do you live in Sacramento?"

"San Francisco." He picked up the check the server put on the table before Becca could grab it.

"You're commuting all the way from there?" It was an hour-and-a-half drive, too long to make twice a day.

He stood instead of answering. "Come on. Let's see how lucky you are."

He wouldn't let her pay for the meal, but took her hand and headed up the escalator to the casino. At the top she stopped him, raising her voice over the din of the machines. "Answer me, please. Are you planning on commuting from San Francisco every day?"

"No." He looked amused.

"Where will you stay?"

"I have a place available." He tugged her toward the nearest bank of slot machines.

"I'm on to you, Gavin Callahan."

His brows went up. "Are you? In what way?"

"You didn't really answer me. Oh, you uttered a sentence about having a place available, but that could mean anything. I suspect you've taken a hotel room. I can't have you doing that." Especially not when he seemed to already be foregoing pay to help her during the week. "You're sneaky, you know?"

He laughed. She loved the sound. But she wasn't going to be swayed by it. "You can stay with me. It'll be easier, anyway. First thing tomorrow, you can buy a bed for the guest room and have it delivered. I'll sleep on the couch tonight."

"Thanks, but it's unnecessary. Julia always has house-sitting jobs available, so even if I wanted to stay with you, I couldn't."

"Oh. Okay." Disappointment hit her full force. The idea of having him around at night had been far too appealing.

"Come on. Try your luck." Before she could even think about arguing, he fed a twenty-dollar bill into the nearest machine and patted the chair seat for her to sit down.

It happened on the eighth pull—Triple, Triple,

Triple. Jackpot! The sound of coins dropping in digitally reproduced beeps seemed almost musical. "How much did I win?" she asked, too excited to figure it out.

"Fifteen hundred."

"I told you I was feeling lucky!" she shouted above the noise around them. She wrapped her arms around his neck and hugged him. After a moment, his arms came around her, his fingertips grazing the upper curve of her rear, an incredibly arousing touch that made her catch her breath. She let go reluctantly when a casino employee appeared to handle the payout.

"For expenses," Becca said, folding all the bills in half. She tried to slip the wad into his suit pocket but it was stitched shut. He saw her dilemma and cocked his head at her in challenge. His only open pockets were those in his pants.

Becca loved challenges, thrived on them, in fact— in business. But the I-dare-you look in his eyes made her bold. She leaned against him, searched blindly for a pocket and tucked the bills inside, making sure they went to the bottom.…

Gavin sucked in a breath, in one sense pleased at her forwardness and yet also aware they were taking a risk that was probably unwise. Yes, they needed to seem married, but if they continued at this rate, they'd hit fever pitch about the time her brothers got to town. If that happened, he and Becca would either be all over each other, or so frustrated they'd be arguing about every little thing.

It was a good thing he couldn't spend the night with her. With anyone. Being alone during the night was critical for him.

"The honeymoon suite's available," one of the drink servers whispered dramatically as she passed by.

Becca stepped back, but was smiling. "Just following orders," she said to Gavin. "You said I should look like a real wife."

"A real wife would've put those bills in her purse."

She laughed. "Well, I'm done here. Are you?"

"That's it? You're not going to play a little longer? You've got luck on your side."

"I know when to fold 'em."

He took her hand and headed toward the parking-lot exit. "You seem like a risk taker to me."

"When the odds are in my favor. I was made VP of operations because I'm a good money manager. I'm expected to keep everyone on budget." She gripped his hand harder. "Thank you for arranging everything today. And for being such a good sport. I—"

"Becca?"

The two young men who'd stepped in front of Gavin and Becca were poster children for the term *nerd,* with their uncombed hair, T-shirts that looked as if they'd been pulled out of a heap, raggedy jeans and trendy sneakers. One was tall and thin, the other short and stocky. But both had eyes filled with intelligence and curiosity.

When Becca failed to introduce them right away, Gavin introduced himself. He wondered how she felt about being caught holding hands.

"I'm Jacob," said the tall one.

"Morgan," said the other. "We work with Becca. Known her since grad school. I've never seen you that dressed up, Bec."

"We just came from a wedding," she said. "What are you two up to?"

"We were in a twenty-four-hour poker tournament. Texas hold 'em," Jacob said.

"How'd you do?" she asked.

They both grinned. "We did okay," Morgan said. "Chip won big."

"Our Chip?" She said to Gavin, "He's our president and CEO."

"Craig's here, too," Jacob added, looking around. "And—"

"Becca," a woman called out.

Gavin watched Becca react to a woman with a short black ponytail as she came in fast for a hug.

"This is Suki," Becca said, looking bemused. "My best friend."

Others approached. Gavin shook hands, endured speculative looks and enjoyed watching Becca be teased by her coworkers. Everyone looked about the same age. Then he remembered her saying that most of them had met in an MBA program at Wharton, then formed their company right after graduation, all of them moving to Sacramento.

The man called Chip, the head honcho, arrived, apparently the last of their group. He was a little more put together than the others. Although he wore jeans, he'd topped it with a sport coat, and his hair was short and neat.

Gavin had chosen Lake Tahoe over Reno for the fake wedding because Reno was closer to his home town of Chance City, therefore with a much stronger possibility of running into people he knew. He hadn't considered that Becca might come up against a similar situation. Now he felt responsible for the jam she was in.

She gave Chip the same story as she had to the others, that they'd just come from a wedding.

"How come we weren't invited?" Chip asked.

She frowned. "Why would I—"

She stopped when Gavin gripped her hand hard, seeing what she apparently hadn't—Chip was eyeing her wedding band. No one else had noticed.

"It was spur-of-the-moment. My fault," Gavin said, subtly moving her finger to touch his ring. "I'm old-fashioned. First things first." Let them make of that what they would, he thought.

"And impatient, apparently," Chip said as everyone else went quiet, including the woman named Suki. As Becca's best friend, she should've been the most talkative, which made him wonder if she'd been in on today's plan.

"I didn't fight it." Becca looked at him as if he were the only man in the world.

"Let us buy you dinner," Chip said, everyone else chiming in.

"They probably want to be alone," Suki said with a wink, which she followed up with a completely different expression directed at Becca, one Gavin couldn't read.

"Are you taking a honeymoon?" Morgan asked.

"Not yet," Becca answered. "I've got that deal going with Keller-Magnuson Industries, and Gavin can't get away at the moment, either."

"Right," Gavin said.

"What do you do?" Chip asked.

"I'm a doctor. Ob-gyn."

Everyone's gaze zeroed in on Becca, whose cheeks flushed but who managed a weak smile.

"Well, at least take tomorrow off," Chip said. "Boss's orders."

"I can't. The teleconference is scheduled for tomorrow morning. You know they've got other offers. It's our only chance."

"But maybe you could let her come home early," Gavin said, trying to look like a romantic newlywed.

"I'll shove her out the door right after the conference." Chip waved a hand. "Come on, gang. Dinner's on me."

They said their goodbyes, then Chip turned back. "Maybe you'll be able to get her to slow down a little."

His words surprised Gavin. He'd figured it was

the business that was driving her to put in such long hours, but Chip seemed to imply otherwise—as if she had a choice and had chosen to put in the extraordinary time. She'd told Gavin that everyone worked long days.

Becca and Gavin went outside to his car, neither of them saying a word until they were settled in and buckled up.

"Ob-gyn, Gavin? Really?"

He held back a grin. "You want me to be able to speak knowledgeably on my profession, don't you?"

"If you'd chosen urology, no one would ask you any questions at all."

He laughed. "So, Suki is your friend who helped you concoct this wild plan."

"The one and only."

"Did she know what we were doing today?"

"*I* didn't even know what we were doing today, remember? I expect to get a call from her any minute—" Her cell phone rang. "No, we didn't really get married," she said instead of hello.

Gavin listened to Becca's side of the conversation as he drove out of the parking lot and onto the main thoroughfare.

"Yes, I'll take tomorrow afternoon off, but that's all...." She gave Gavin a quick look. "Of course not, Suki. I repeat. We did not get married....I know, but just because we're wearing rings doesn't mean that...I agree, he is....Tuesday, I promise....Okay, bye." She ended the call and tucked the phone into her purse.

"You agree I'm what?" he asked.

"I don't want to give you a swelled head."

He gave her a curious look, wondering if she realized what she'd said. "Aw, come on, Becca. Tell me."

She sighed. "Okay. She said you're cute."

He didn't buy it. She was squeezing her hands together, a gesture he was coming to identify with her avoiding telling the truth.

"What did she *really* say, Becca?"

She didn't roll her eyes, but came close to it. "That you're hot, okay? Are you happy now?"

"Well, yeah. That's a whole lot better than being called cute. Babies and puppies are cute. It might complicate things, though."

"That Suki thinks you're hot? Why?"

He curved his hand over her knee. "Because you agreed with her."

She grabbed his shirt cuff, moved his hand over to his own leg then dropped it. "Don't get all cocky, Gavin."

"I'll try not to, but you seem to have that effect on me."

She finally laughed, as if she'd been holding it in and couldn't for a second longer, the sound spilling from her almost musically. He liked her. A lot. He didn't like lying, but he understood she had what she considered good reasons. For his part, he tried not to overthink it all.

Something else occurred to him. "Are any of your coworkers in touch with your brothers?"

"No. Wait. Maybe. Chip's been talking to Eric about doing business with us. I didn't ask Chip not to say anything...." She grabbed her cell phone. "No reception now that we're away from town." She tapped her phone against her chin.

"I can turn around and go back," Gavin said. "We haven't been on the road that long."

"It's Sunday. I doubt they would be in touch. I'll call as soon as I get reception. I think we'll be okay."

Their playful mood shattered, they continued down the mountain a long time until she got enough bars to call. She had to leave a message.

"Hey, Chip. I know this pretty much goes without saying, but of course I want to be the one to tell my brothers about Gavin, so just in case you talk to Eric, don't say anything, okay? Call me when you get this, please. Thanks!"

But by the time Gavin left her loft that evening, Chip hadn't called back. And Becca was a mess.

Gavin wasn't in such great shape himself. He appreciated having something to do, but the roles they were playing hadn't seemed real until he'd had to pretend in front of her friends.

It was late when he drove to his hotel, checked in and unpacked, his mind whirling relentlessly. His "recent legal problem," as Julia Swanson had so nicely called it, wasn't really over. Would never be over. Yes, he'd been exonerated, but that was the least of it. Lives had been irrevocably changed—not just his. In fact, his mattered the least. The lawsuit itself didn't weigh on him—the final result for him, for all of them, would've been the same had the legal outcome gone the other way. Only the people mattered, and all the pain everyone endured, would continue to endure.

He doubted himself as a doctor now when he'd been so sure before. So cocksure.

Now he was on the run from dealing with it, and not handling it well.

Except when he was with Becca, who gave him entirely different things to think about. He hadn't figured her out yet, wanted to know what drove her to work so hard. She was the second-highest-ranking employee in her company. No one got that job without doing more than almost everyone else.

She was a puzzle he hoped to solve.

Chapter Five

"I know, I know. I don't look like a happy new bride," Becca said after opening the door to Gavin the next morning. "I didn't sleep much."

"From everything you've told me about your brothers, if Chip had called Eric, you would've heard about it by now." Gavin laid a hand along her face, looking into her eyes. "Worry doesn't help. Bagels do, however." He held up a large sack. "Bacon, orange juice and coffee, too."

"I'm not sure I can eat." Her stomach was full of worry, no matter what Gavin said, but she followed him into the kitchen, grateful for his presence. He made quick work of putting food on plates as she sat at the counter and sipped at her coffee.

"What time is your conference?" he asked.

"Eleven."

"Are you prepared for it?"

"Pretty much. I do this a couple of times a month. It's fairly standard." She eyed the plate he set in front of her, picked up a piece of bacon and bit into it. "Good," she mumbled. "Thanks. What are your plans?"

He sat next to her. "Grocery shopping this morning. And since you'll be home this afternoon, I'll leave some of the paper sorting to when you're here. Fair warning—we're going to be ruthless. When we've winnowed down, we can figure out how many file cabinets you need."

She swallowed a lump in her throat. She rebelled at her brothers taking care of her, but was finding it easy to let Gavin take over. Maybe she'd reached the end of her rope and was finally acknowledging it. Plus she didn't feel a need to impress him with her competency. He'd known from the moment he walked through her door that she'd lost control of her life at some point.

"I know you pick up food well, but do you cook?" she asked.

"I have survival skills. Figured I'd invest in a cookbook today and give a few things a try. How hard can it be?"

"I guess we'll find out. I do own a fire extinguisher," she added.

He smiled. "Duly noted."

"And my brothers have no expectations when it comes to food and me."

"So you've said. Filling in the blanks here, Becca, it's safe to say they do have expectations about your happiness. They want to know you're being well taken care of, even though you've taken care of yourself just fine. They sound old-fashioned and loving. You asked me to play a role. I don't do anything halfway."

She wanted to kiss him so much her mouth ached. Since he'd kissed her at the altar, she'd relived the moment over and over.

"Feel better?" he asked.

She blinked. "What?"

He pointed to her empty plate.

"You make me forget my troubles," she said honestly. Her stomach had relaxed, too, at least for as long as it had taken to eat. "I guess I should get to work. Thank you for breakfast—and the company."

He followed her to the door. "If you need me, I'm a phone call away."

The lump in her throat came back. "Thank you," she said, trying not to let on how his kindness affected her. She could get used to this—to *him*—in a hurry.

Chip was the only one in the office when Becca arrived. She set her briefcase on her desk then waited for him to end his phone call before she went to his office.

"Come in, Becca. Have a seat," he said, leaning on his elbows. "You look like you had a long night."

His lack of a smile indicated he wasn't teasing her. "You didn't return my call," she said.

"No." He angled back, steepling his fingers at his chin.

"You didn't talk to Eric, did you?"

"I did."

The air went out of her. "What did—"

"A week ago, Becca. Your brother talked to me a week ago about how you'd eloped, expecting that I already knew. I kept waiting for you to tell me, all of us, but you never did. And now it seems you got married *yesterday*. I don't know what to believe or why it's even happening. This is not the Becca Sheridan I've known all these years."

She squeezed her hands together, not knowing what to say. He was right. She had no defense.

"We've been friends a long time—all six of us who started this business. Until now, I've never doubted anything about you," Chip said.

"I have reasons."

"Are you married?" he asked when she didn't elaborate.

"I'll explain everything, Chip. Soon. I know I'm putting you in a difficult position, because you're also friends with Eric, and you've just started some business deal with him. I'm sorry, but I can't tell you anything more."

She needed to talk to Gavin. She needed some levelheaded advice. Maybe she needed to come clean with her brothers, not take this ruse one step further.

Of course then they would *really* question her judgment. "In the meantime, please just trust me. It has nothing to do with the business."

He said nothing for a few long seconds, and then he sighed, the tone one of frustration. "What choice do I have? I'll keep your confidence. For now." He gestured her toward the door. "You've got a conference to prepare for."

Becca retreated to her office, shutting the door behind her. She was tempted to call Gavin but didn't. She'd gotten herself into this mess. She needed to get herself out of it.

He should've bought the cookbook before grocery shopping, Gavin realized as he thumbed through the collection of recipes. Would've made much more sense that way.

He heard Becca's key in the lock, then the door opened. She looked worse than when she'd left.

"Bad day?" he asked as she set her briefcase by the front door.

"You could say that." She dropped onto the couch.

"Your conference didn't go well?"

She rubbed her face. "It was fine. I'd be surprised if we don't get the contract, but we won't know for a few days, I imagine."

He sat on the sofa, not at the opposite end, but closer to the middle. "What happened, Becca?"

"Chip's known for a week that I'd eloped. Eric

brought it up to him, and Chip's been waiting for me to tell him."

"And then he thought we'd gotten married yesterday," Gavin said.

"I need to tell my brothers the truth," she said. "If Chip no longer has faith in my integrity, how do you think my brothers will feel?" She shoved herself up. "It was such a stupid plan."

"You were being a loving sister. You want them to stop worrying about you. That's not stupid."

"Or so I'd convinced myself. And look at this place," she said, gesturing broadly. "Underneath all the boxes and stacks of paper is nothing. I haven't even bothered to furnish it, much less make it a home. I haven't invited anyone here except Suki. Well, a couple of my brothers right after I moved, when I still had an excuse for the boxes. My mother would be horrified at how I'm living. It's a mess. *I'm* a mess."

"It's cluttered, but it's not dirty," he said, moving toward her.

"Only because I have a housecleaner once a month! And I'm gone more than I'm home. What does that tell you?" She pressed a hand to her mouth. "Excuse me." She ran past him, heading toward the master bedroom.

"Becca, stop." He caught up with her, grabbed her, pulled her into his arms. "Let it out. It's okay. Just let it out."

She shoved against him halfheartedly then

wrapped her arms around him and cried as if she'd been holding it in for years. Maybe she had been. Maybe this had to do with her parents, too, since she'd said her mother would be horrified at how she was living. He didn't try to shush her, although the sound of her sobs was heartbreaking—and further evidence of long-buried emotion.

She felt good in his arms. Right. And as long as he was being honest—it felt good to be held in return. He hadn't been this close to a woman in a long time, and Becca fit, perfectly. So perfectly that he didn't let go of her after she stopped crying and tucked her face against his neck, her breaths hot and shaky.

"I got you all wet," she said, not trying to get away from him.

"Careful. I might melt." He tightened his hold.

She laughed a little then settled again even closer. "Thank you."

"I'm glad I could help." He didn't want to let go, either, although they would have to. Any minute now…

Becca knew she should move away, but he was rubbing her back up and down, slowly, soothingly. Her muscles turned to mush. She almost fell asleep. Then she remembered why she'd been so wound up to start with. She eased away, went into the kitchen and dampened a paper towel to pat her face.

"I should call Eric and get it over with," she said. "Tell him the truth."

"I've been giving that some thought. I feel pretty strongly that you should hold off for now." Gavin leaned against the counter, watching her. No, *examining* her was a better term for how he was looking at her, as if she was under a microscope. "You made the decision to pretend you were married for certain reasons. Valid or not, it's done. So why don't we just continue on here until the weekend? I can still help you get your place in good shape. We can get your life organized so that you feel good about that. Then you can decide on Saturday what to tell your brothers. Better to do it in person and with all of them at once, anyway, rather than making four phone calls. I don't think you need to rush into a decision."

He was offering a stall she could rationalize well enough, so she grabbed it. "But what about everyone at work? They all think I'm married—except Chip, who's totally confused about it and kind of angry. And Suki, of course, who knows the truth."

"Can you ignore the subject with them for the rest of the week?"

"I don't know. Maybe. I've never been in this kind of situation before."

"I would hope not." He smiled.

"I mean lying to my friends and family."

"I know. Why not just tell Chip the truth?"

"And remove all doubt that I've gone over some edge of sanity? No, thanks. I'd rather come up with a plausible explanation when this is over. He'll forgive me." At least she thought he would.

Gavin pushed away from the counter. "Why don't you change out of your work clothes. I'll fix some sandwiches, then we can get started on your loft."

"Okay." She retreated to her bedroom. The mirror reflected her blotchy face and swollen eyes, but she felt pretty good, considering.

Except for the escalating lies…and that attraction to Gavin that kept getting in the way. Starting with how gorgeous he was, moving on to his powers of perception and then his great sense of humor.

She'd met men like him before, men content to live day to day, without plans for their future. They were generally easygoing and likable. But Gavin had the potential for so much more. He was educated and smart—

And it wasn't her problem, not at all. He'd be gone from her life soon, leaving her better for having known him.

Becca changed clothes then went out to join him.

"Lie down," he said, indicating the sofa.

"Am I about to be psychoanalyzed, Dr. Callahan?" she asked, but doing what he ordered without asking why. She figured he wouldn't answer, anyway.

"Please. We're friends. Call me Sigmund. Now close your eyes."

Smiling, she did so, then felt something cold being placed on her eyelids.

"Cucumber slices, for the swelling," he said. "Good thing I went shopping today, hmm?"

She felt instantly soothed and relaxed. "Good boy," she said as one would say to a puppy.

"Careful."

She laughed. "I may fall asleep."

"I seem to have that effect on you."

She peeled up the cucumber slices and looked at his smiling, caring face. "You might be surprised at the effect you have on me," she said, then let the slices drop back into place, amazed at her brashness, but not about to apologize for the truth.

She jumped when she felt his hands flatten against the sides of her thighs. Moving his palms in circles, he made his way down her legs, his fingers seeming to come along for the ride, not pressing into her, just sliding along, the heels of his hands doing most of the work. When he reached her feet, he massaged them through her socks, digging his thumbs into all the right places until she moaned.

She should make him stop. At the least she should take off the makeshift eye mask and look at him, but the sensation of darkness, the not knowing what he would do next was too intriguing, too tempting to give up—especially when he moved his competent hands to her shoulders then dragged them down her arms until he reached her hands, giving them the same thorough treatment as her feet.

He let his hands travel back up her arms to her shoulders, kneading them, his fingers working the tight muscles, his palms resting on her chest. If she'd had much in the way of breasts, he would've been cushioned by that flesh.

"Not much there," she murmured aloud, continuing to be surprised by what she told him.

"There's plenty."

She didn't know what to say to that. In truth, she was comfortable with her body, with her small breasts, but she knew men usually preferred...more.

He put his mouth on hers. She hadn't expected it, hadn't felt him drawing near, yet she welcomed it as he moved his lips over hers leisurely, enticingly. His tongue sought entry, but still he kept things slow when what she suddenly wanted was speed and heat, the hunger for him intense.

Too intense. She wasn't ready for this. Not now. Not yet. She didn't want to know what he was like in bed, because she figured he'd be perfection—generous and satisfying, as he was in every other aspect in life. She didn't want to be left with that memory when he walked away.

"Stop," she whispered. "Please."

He released her. She lifted the cucumber slices away and looked at him, at his expression that told her little, only that maybe her quick change in mood seemed a little crazy to him. She wanted to share, but she couldn't. Not yet.

"Hungry?" he asked. "Sandwiches are ready."

Hungry? "Starved," she said, standing, feeling a little light-headed then finding her bearings again.

"You look better," he said later, after they'd eaten.

She nodded. She felt better, too. Energized and aroused—an invigorating combination. "I'm ready to get to work."

Hours later they called in an order for pizza, plopped onto the couch and surveyed her living room. As soon as they recycled the magazines and other papers they'd stacked by her front door, there would be little left to take up space.

"I knew I didn't have much furniture," she said. "But I thought I had more than this."

"Do you have anything in storage somewhere?"

"This is all of it. I've always traveled light. I also gave away most of my old pieces when I moved in here, wanting to start fresh."

"Do you have ideas about furnishing the rooms?"

"I'd like it to look good. A place I could bring not just friends but business associates to, but I'm so bad at decorating, Gavin. I have no vision for the big picture."

"How about the little picture?"

"What do you mean?"

Gavin walked into the guest room and came out with a box. "I came across these today. Something from your childhood, I imagine."

She peered into the box as he held the lid open, but she didn't take anything out. She knew what was inside—about fifty figurines of dogs made of all different kinds of materials, from ceramic to plastic to metal. Breeds of all kinds, too. From three inches tall to a half inch.

"Would you want these displayed?" he asked.

"I can't see them fitting the decor."

"Does it matter? If they're special, they'll fit."

"No. They're kid stuff."

"Yet you've kept them."

"They're from my past. I don't need them displayed." *Or the memories associated with them.* She knew she was being abrupt and evasive, but she couldn't talk about it with him.

He was quiet a long time. "My sister Shana is pretty good at decorating, apparently. If you want, I can get her involved."

"You are the gift that keeps on giving," Becca said with a sigh, relieved he'd stopped pushing. "Yes. By all means, yes." She would say anything at this point to end his questions.

He pulled out his phone, searched for a number.

"You don't have to take care of it right this second," she said, feeling guilty for turning over the task to him and his sister, but also wishing he would just rest for a few minutes. He'd been teaching her how to do that, yet couldn't always do the same himself.

Sometimes he seemed…well, *haunted,* for lack of a better word. He retreated into himself, not talking, emptying boxes as if on autopilot.

"We can't delay, Becca. This'll take a few days, and I don't know what kind of time she has available."

He held up a finger. "Hey, Shana….Good, how about you?…And Emma?" He laughed. "Careful what you wish for. She'll be running before you know it, and you'll never catch up with her. Hey, what's your work schedule this week?…Because I've got a decorating job for you, if you're interested. A big job. Actually a *fast* job. It needs to be done by Saturday morning.… Yes, the client from the agency.…"

He tipped the phone down a little. "What style?"

"Comfortable contemporary, I guess. Not a lot of knickknacks."

"Did you hear that, Shana?" He finished up the conversation then set down the phone.

The doorbell rang. Becca beat him to the door, paid for the pizza then inhaled the scent as she carried it to the kitchen counter.

"I bought beer," Gavin said. "Want one?"

"Thanks. I take it your sister is free tomorrow?"

"*Only* tomorrow, so we'll be hauling through town trying to find the right items. Plus Shana is as picky about price as she is about quality. You'll get bargains."

Becca stared at the countertop, her throat aching. "Nobody's ever done anything like this before. I mean, my brothers did things for me, overdid things, but it wasn't the same. I don't know how to describe it."

"Probably more accurately—you've never let anyone. I'd wager your friend Suki offered to help you with this place."

"Many times." They sat at the counter, each grabbing a slice of a combo pizza.

"Why haven't you accepted?" he asked.

She tried to keep it light. "I'm sure your alter ego, Freud, would know. Avoidance, probably, but I don't know of what."

"It *is* a way of avoiding personal relationships," he said, thoughtfully. "If your home is a disaster, you don't invite anyone over. You don't let dates pick you up or bring you home."

He was watching her for a reaction. "There might be some truth to that. Plus the fact I'm busy."

"Which is a choice you made."

"Well, aren't you Mr. Insight?"

"Tell me this, Becca. What excuse will you have when our 'marriage' has ended and your home is acceptable for company?"

He was relentless, and she was annoyed. "That's enough, Gavin."

"Don't you want to meet someone? Fall in love? The whole marriage-and-kids thing?"

"Do you?"

"Of course. Sometime."

"Of course," she repeated, going cold. "Well, not me. I don't want that at all."

His brows went up. "Why not?"

"You're smart. You figure it out." She couldn't keep talking about it. She flipped the lid down on the pizza box and shoved it at him. "I think you need to go now. Please."

It took her a good five minutes after the door shut behind him before she moved. When she did, it was to go to the bedroom to look at the photographs on her dresser.

She didn't find comfort there, but resolve. And that was enough to keep her going.

At midnight, Gavin was still pacing the floor of his hotel room, doubly grateful now that he'd turned down Becca's offer to stay at her place for the week. He'd needed to be away from her. Far, far away.

But sleep eluded him even more than usual.

He dragged a chair in front of the window, mesmerized by lights dotting the dark sky, whether buildings, planes or stars. The view was familiar now, his having spent several nights there, but it still captivated him.

She had no desire to be a wife and mother. The idea never would've occurred to him.

He'd been so shocked, he hadn't thought through his response. He shouldn't have questioned her. Shouldn't have boxed her into a corner about such a personal decision.

You figure it out, she'd said, as if he could.

Hints. He needed hints. A heartbreak of some kind, obviously. Something that had set her on her current path of working too much and too hard. Of running away from something. If she stopped, she would have to face it. And this was something she really didn't want to face. What?

The dog figurines were tied in somehow, too, he was sure of it.

He rubbed his hands over his face. The only thing he knew for sure was the fact she'd just gotten even more interesting.

Chapter Six

Early the next morning Gavin drove the short distance to Becca's place. Shana pulled into a visitor parking space right next to him. After ten years of wandering the world, she'd settled down, was all grown up now. The fact she'd shown up so early said a lot about how responsible she'd become.

He'd hesitated to recommend her to Becca. Shana wasn't a trained or experienced decorator. To his knowledge she'd only helped decorate Dixie's salon and spa, and her apartment. But both had impressed him, and Becca needed someone right now.

"I hope you're hungry," he said as they moved toward the elevator. "I brought breakfast for three."

"I could eat, thanks. I dropped Emma off with

Aggie, but didn't have time for breakfast myself." She eyed him thoughtfully. "So, this job turned out to be more than you originally signed up for?"

"By my choice. As you pointed out, I had nothing else to do, so I volunteered."

"I'm glad and grateful you took the job, Gavin. Julia was thrilled, too."

Gavin pushed the up button for the elevator. "She's interesting. Becca, I mean."

"Apparently."

He glanced at her in question.

"You're already wearing a wedding ring." Her Callahan-green eyes, which all three siblings had inherited, fixed on him with curiosity and humor.

The fact that neither he nor Becca remembered to take off the rings was something the oft-referenced Freud would've had something to say about, Gavin thought.

"We both are wearing rings. Just getting used to it." Another lie. He'd actually forgotten he had it on.

The door to the fourth floor whooshed opened. "I want details," she said, following him down the hall.

"I'm sure you've been asked for discretion in your own jobs for At Your Service." He looked at her in time to see her nod. "Same here. I'll let Becca decide what to tell you."

A few seconds later they were inside the loft and

introductions made. Gavin headed directly to the kitchen to set out breakfast for everyone, grateful for the reprieve of Shana's presence. After last night's discussion, Becca seemed normal, but then, they had company.

While they ate, Becca and Shana conferred about the plan. When they were done eating, he loaded their plates into the dishwasher, listening to them discuss the budget and Shana's fee, getting that business out of the way.

"It's seven-thirty," he said, breaking into their conversation as they moved away from the task at hand.

"Already?" Becca grabbed her briefcase and started out the door. "Shana, thank you so much for this. You have no idea the pressure you've taken off me."

"I'm happy to do it."

"Do you have a second, Gavin?" Becca asked, indicating he should come into the hall with her.

He followed.

"You've barely looked at me," she said when the door shut behind them and they walked toward the elevator.

"I figured you would want to spend your time talking with Shana."

"That's all?"

He didn't like the way her eyes probed his, searching for more. He punched the down button for her. "I figure you'd be sorry that you told me what you did last night."

The elevator door opened. She stepped inside but held her hand across the door. "I'm not. And I don't want to talk about it again."

Her decision to stay single pained her, he realized. Deeply. *What drove you to choose that, Becca?*

He leaned over and kissed her, as if he had no control over his actions. Maybe he didn't.

"Have a good day, honey," he said, attempting to make her laugh, to lighten the moment.

But as the door closed, she only looked confused.

Join the club, he thought as he walked back to her unit. He found Shana sketching, a measuring tape in hand. He became her assistant, and she kindly asked no personal questions.

He didn't let on about his doubts she could handle a job this big. But more than most people, she needed someone's vote of confidence, and he needed to give it.

He hadn't spent this much time with Shana in years—for as long as he could remember, actually. Maybe ever. He'd thought their sister Dixie had gotten all the organizational skills in the family, but Shana surprised him. She came up with a plan before they left the loft, and by the end of the very long day, she'd ordered everything except a light to go over the new dining-room table, and a few accessories. Deliveries would start the next day. She would come back Friday night to stage the rooms.

"This has been fun," Shana said as they dropped onto the sofa to share chips and salsa at the end of the day.

"I don't know how you keep track of it all. My head's spinning."

"I already see it finished. There's a spot right over there—" she pointed to the wall behind where the dining set would go "—that will need filling. I could pick out something, but I think she should. Maybe she has some art that would fit."

"She has photo albums and pictures in frames."

"It needs something colorful. A painting, maybe, but a sculptural piece with some depth is better. A touch of burnt orange would be good, too, to go with some of the other accessories. Can you take her shopping?" She set her heels on the coffee table and crossed her ankles.

"I guess."

"A new glass-tile backsplash in the kitchen would be perfect, just along the far wall. It's a pretty small space, so it's doable," she said, looking around. "And she really should paint the living room/dining room space, but I don't think there's time for either of those things by Saturday. It's almost impossible to line someone up that fast. I'm totally booked, or I would do it myself."

"I could do it."

Shana laughed.

Gavin took offense. "Why is that so funny?"

She picked up his hand and ran her fingers over it. "Soft. Smooth. Hands that don't do manual labor."

It was all the challenge he needed. "You pick out the paint and tile. I'll have it done by Friday at noon."

"This I've gotta see." She grinned. "What are we betting?"

"What do you want, if you win?"

"A tune-up for my car."

She continued to smile but her unfrivolous request stabbed at him. She traveled a lot of miles every day, almost always commuting to Sacramento, two hours, round-trip. She should be driving something reliable, not the heap she owned. Barring that, it should at least be maintained well.

"Deal," he said. "And if I win, you owe me a thorough cleaning of my place in the city."

"Well, that's win-win for me," she said. "At the very least, I'll get to spend a couple of days in San Francisco. Let's shake on it." She stood. "And on that note, I'll take off before you fully realize your generous mistake. I'll stop by the store on my way out of town to choose the paint and the tile. If they don't deliver, maybe Becca can pick it all up at lunch tomorrow."

She almost skipped out the door. Gavin grabbed

his cell phone and placed a call to Landon Kincaid, a licensed contractor and real-estate developer Gavin had known since high school. Kincaid and Shana had a somewhat touchy relationship. Gavin didn't know the source of the conflict, because they hadn't known each other very long, but maybe he could use it to his advantage.

"Kincaid? Hey, it's Gavin Callahan."

"How's it going, Gavin?"

"I seem to have gotten myself into a bit of a jam. I just made a bet with Shana that I know I can't win on my own. It's your area of expertise, however. Care to help?" He explained the situation to Kincaid, who didn't answer right away.

"I can't be part of a plan to cheat her, Gavin."

"I'm not asking you to. I'm going to tell her she was right, that I was completely incompetent and so I asked you to help. She'll win the bet, no matter what."

"Why go to that extreme?"

"Because I want to give her something she wants. She only asked for a tune-up for her car. This way she'll win the bet, but it won't seem like charity, which we both know she wouldn't accept, even from me."

"I'm in."

When Becca arrived home a couple hours later, Gavin had marinated chicken breasts to grill, put together a green salad and had asparagus ready to roast in the oven. It was a simple meal, not much of a stretch, even for him.

"Smells good," Becca said as she made her way to the bar counter.

"Chocolate-chip cookies."

"Seriously?"

"Don't be too impressed," he said. "It's slice and bake."

"It's more than I've done. Thanks." She accepted a glass of Merlot. "Careful, Gavin. I could get used to this." Hesitancy marked her words and actions, as if she had no idea what to expect from him and didn't know how to behave.

"How was your day?" he asked, urging her toward the couch.

"Strange. Everyone asked questions without using actual words. I got a lot of raised eyebrows, followed by pauses, as if I would fill in the blanks. And Chip's not speaking to me unless absolutely necessary. And then two potentially huge clients contacted us out of the blue, which is wonderful, and which is also why I'm late. So, how did you and Shana do?"

"She's a human tornado. I never knew that about her. I could barely keep up. It means your place will be ready to go by Friday night—unless something doesn't get delivered. But I wouldn't want to be on the receiving end of a call or visit from Shana, should that happen." He smiled at the image. "I remember her as this kind of loner kid who said little and stayed in her room a lot. She's become a mature, competent woman. Becoming a mother probably had a lot to do with that."

He angled toward Becca. "It got me looking at you through your brothers' eyes. Until they see you in action in some way, as I did with Shana, they'll always think of you as their kid sister. A girl, not a woman."

"Maybe we could have a take-your-brothers-to-work day at the office," she said, seeming to relax finally.

"My guess is they'd be as surprised as I was about Shana. I'd just never given it any thought. She's been frozen in time for me, I see that now." The timer went off. He got up to take the cookies out of the oven. "Maybe it's not a matter of your brothers seeing you in action at work but the fact you'll have your house in order that'll make them realize that you're grown up. It should help, anyway."

"I sure hope so. What did you tell Shana about us?"

"As little as possible." He moved the cookies to wire racks to cool. "She knows we're pretending to be married. Plus, I forgot to take off the ring. You, too, I see."

"At work they think I *am* married."

He grabbed his wineglass and returned to the couch. "Would you like to see the schematic Shana came up with or do you want to be surprised?"

"Do you think I might not like something?"

"Far from it. We also have a homework assignment to choose a decorative piece for that wall. Maybe tomorrow after dinner?"

"Most of the galleries close at five o'clock, but I could take a long lunch, if that works for you."

"I need to be here. The delivery window from all of the stores is from nine to five."

Every time he looked at her, he felt guilty. She was too quiet, for one thing, and her eyes weren't sparkling as they had at times. He'd opened some kind of Pandora's box for her last night. She may be trying to ignore it, but it hadn't completely gone back into hiding yet.

When dinner was ready, they sat at the counter to eat. In silence. He couldn't figure out how to change the mood.

"Let's go for a walk," he said after the meal ended. "We can window-shop the galleries. Maybe you'll see the right piece for that spot on the wall."

Becca lived in a largely residential community in a city famous for its trees and old Victorian houses. Surprisingly her contemporary high-rise building suited the long-settled location. Surrounding her building were boutiques and galleries, bars and clubs, and casual dining to please every palate and price range. The second Saturday of every month brought an art walk and thousands of people into the area.

"I can probably find the right piece if I wait for

Second Saturday," she said as they walked out into the early-evening air, the sun just setting in hazy brushstrokes of purples and oranges. "Do you think Shana would be upset if I left it until then?"

"Upset, no. But I imagine she'll fill it with something in the meantime. She talked about needing a balance of color there." He took Becca's hand, felt her surprise, then she seemed to relax.

They wandered for almost an hour, then came across an amazing wall sculpture in a gallery window, a copper-and-bronze stylized recreation of the Tower Bridge, one of Sacramento's landmarks. A setting sun gave the metal an orange glow.

"I hope Shana agrees it works," Becca said, "because I love it. I could easily spend time sitting at my new dining-room table and seeing it on the wall."

"Let's find out," Gavin said. He pulled out his cell phone and took a picture, then emailed it to his sister. Shana replied a second later. "'Perfect. Buy it.'"

"I'll call the store tomorrow and have the sculpture delivered," Becca said. "Unless it's too expensive."

They returned to her building, their assignment complete.

"I think I'll leave you here," Gavin said as they stood at the elevator bank.

Becca's stomach clenched. Maybe they hadn't settled things, after all. "You don't want any cookies?" she asked to cover her surprise.

"Do you plan to eat them all tonight?"

"You never know."

He laughed. "I'll take my chances. Plus, I didn't use up all the dough." A pinging sound indicated the arrival of the elevator. "Good night, Becca."

"Thank you for everything," she said, feeling lost. She really hadn't expected him to leave so early.

She started to get into the elevator. He started to walk away. Simultaneously they turned to look at each other and then hesitated. Becca made the first move, saying his name, letting the elevator door shut. She moved toward him. He welcomed her with open arms, wrapped her up tight. His lips devoured hers, his tongue seeking and tasting, arousing. She groaned at the heat permeating her as their bodies touched.

"Come upstairs with me," she murmured against his mouth, aware of their public situation.

"I can't," he said, although intensifying the kiss, taking complete charge for a good, long time.

"Why?" she finally managed to ask.

"Because I really *want* to."

She waited to see if he would add anything, but that was it. She understood what he was saying, but she wished he didn't have so much willpower.

And was also grateful for it.

"I'll see you in the morning," she said. The elevator door opened the instant she touched the up button.

This time she didn't look back.

After all, a dozen chocolate-chip cookies awaited her. She didn't intend to leave a single one.

Chapter Seven

"**W**hat makes you think you're just gonna be my gofer?" Landon Kincaid asked Gavin the next morning after draping tarps over the living-room furniture in preparation for the work ahead.

"I don't know anything about painting," Gavin said.

"You're about to learn."

"I'm paying *you* to do the job."

"I dropped everything to help you out."

The two men, about the same height and build, stared at each other, not in anger but with a touch of humor. Both were used to being in charge. Neither backed down often.

"It's a life skill you should have," Kincaid said, crouching to pry open a paint can.

"Not as long as there are professional painters in the world," Gavin said.

"Maybe you'd like to set the backsplash tile, instead?" Kincaid asked mildly.

Gavin raised both hands. "Uncle."

Kincaid grunted, poured paint into two roller trays then gave Gavin instructions, along with a hands-on demonstration. Throughout the morning, new household purchases were delivered and tarped. Music blared—country, which was Kincaid's choice—to cover their lack of conversation, not because they didn't like each other, but because they had little in common. Not only had they taken entirely different career paths, Kincaid still lived in Chance City, Gavin's hometown, a place he avoided.

At one o'clock, they were finishing up the living room/dining room area when Becca popped in. Gavin hadn't told her they would be painting, hoping she would come home tonight to freshly done rooms.

"So much for surprises," he muttered as she moved into the room, smiling, taking it all in, a string-tied cardboard package in her hands.

"I love the color. Shana is *good*." She spotted Kincaid then and extended her hand, balancing her package on the floor. "Hi, I'm Becca Sheridan."

"Kincaid."

"You work fast."

His eyes took on enough mischief to worry Gavin. "I've had help."

"Gavin? Really?"

"Why are you so shocked? I'm good with my hands." He decided to change the subject before Kincaid said something that might complicate things. "What's in the box?"

She hefted it. "The bridge sculpture. I'll get some scissors."

"I can open it for you," Kincaid said, grabbing a box opener from his tool chest, making quick work of it. The cardboard fell aside, revealing a piece even more beautiful than it had looked in the front-window display.

Gavin held it up in the spot it would find its home.

"Perfect," Becca said, clasping her hands under her chin, admiring her find.

Gavin could see she'd finally gotten excited about her loft truly becoming her home. Even without his help at this point, she would finish it.

He also couldn't look at her without remembering their kiss in front of the elevator last night. Mutual need, mutual demand. It was getting harder and harder for him to stay out of her bed.

"You must be a magician," she said to Gavin but turning to include Kincaid. "I've heard that getting a craftsman can take days, even weeks. Or did Shana arrange it?"

"Kincaid and I went to high school together. He took pity on me. I sounded desperate."

"True," Kincaid said. "It's been…entertaining watching him perform manual labor."

"What *are* you good at?" she asked Gavin.

"I'm becoming a jack-of-all-trades," he said, putting an arm around her shoulders to guide her into the kitchen, thus ending the conversation.

She was eyeing him, her expression caught between curiosity and amusement, as if she was on to his vague explanations. "I love the way the living room is starting to look. Shana is a genius. She must be in big demand as a designer."

When Gavin didn't respond, she left the kitchen and crossed through the ghost town of tarped furniture to the front door to return to work. "Kincaid, thank you so much."

The door shut behind her. Gavin looked at Kincaid, who crossed his arms and cocked his head. "She was wearing a wedding band," he said.

Gavin turned on the faucet to wash his hands, making noise instead of answering.

"And isn't it interesting," Kincaid continued casually as he wandered into the kitchen, "there's a matching man's ring right there on the counter."

Gavin gave him a look but said nothing. Those rings were causing major problems. He'd gotten as far as taking his off while he painted, but why hadn't he hidden it? There had to be a reason, one he didn't want to acknowledge, even to himself.

"Did you get married, Gavin?"

"No."

"So that ring belongs to another man? Her husband?" He leaned against the counter. "I remember your Don Juan reputation in high school. I would've thought you'd outgrown that by now."

"It's not what you think. And I'm not at liberty to explain at the moment. We're not sleeping together."

"You want to. So does she."

That was a good thing, Gavin decided. Her brothers would believe them—if she didn't decide to tell them the truth instead. "How long until the paint is dry?"

Kincaid laughed, a rare sound for him. "Okay, I get it. None of my business."

"True, but also a legitimate question. I'd like to move some of the stuff that arrived today into place before Becca gets home."

"It'll be dry enough by the time we're done with the tile."

"We? Really, Kincaid, I don't consider tiling a life skill."

"I do," he said cheerfully. "What're you griping about, anyway? It's an eighteen-inch-by-six-foot space. I'll do the grouting."

"Damn right you will."

Gavin found himself enjoying the tiling, especially seeing such a big change in a short time. The kitchen sparkled as if dressed in jewels. By six o'clock, everything was done and the furniture moved into place according to Shana's master plan. Gavin and Kincaid leaned against the counter bar enjoying a beer and admiring their work. At least, Gavin was. It was nothing new for Kincaid.

"I may have given you grief today," Gavin said, "but I appreciate everything you did, especially how fast you came. I know you're always in demand."

"No problem." He took a long sip as he glanced at Gavin. "Does Shana have enough money to get by? Seems like she's putting in a lot of hours."

"She also commutes two hours a day. Sacramento's the only place she can get consistent work."

"It's got to be hard, leaving Emma behind with a sitter every day."

Gavin nodded. It bothered him, too, but when he'd offered her financial assistance, she'd turned him down cold, determined to make it on her own. "I figure that's the hardest thing for her. But as for funds, lots of people invite them for meals, Aggie babysits for free, as do a few others. Shana seems to be managing. And I think if she were desperate, she would let me help her."

"What about your parents?"

"Mom is in touch. Dad hasn't forgiven her."

"Idiot." The word came out like a curse and hung in the air for a few seconds.

What could Gavin say to that, anyway? He agreed. His father was a narrow-minded idiot who was missing the opportunity to know his granddaughter, as well as enjoy his daughter's company. Shana had become a steady, responsible woman. She deserved a second chance.

Kincaid set his empty bottle in the sink. "Let me know if you need anything else done."

"Thanks. I'll help carry your stuff to your truck."

Gavin returned to the loft fifteen minutes later, appreciating the fresh, new look to the place as he walked through the front door, even though it wasn't completely furnished yet. He needed a shower, yet he wanted to see Becca's reaction when she got home. The problem was she came home a different time each night and he was afraid that if he changed, he'd miss her arrival.

He did have a change of clothes in his car. He could use her second bathroom, get in, get out…

He retrieved his clothes, took the world's fastest shower, put on his jeans, then was towel drying his hair as he went into the living room, making sure she hadn't come home. All clear.

He headed back to the bathroom then heard her key in the lock. The front door swung open. She stood still, taking in the room.

"What do you think?" he asked.

She jumped, apparently not having realized he'd been standing in the bathroom doorway watching her….

"It's…" Becca's gaze landed on him, shirtless, messy haired, barefoot, reminding her once again of a perfect sculpture. He had broad shoulders and an interesting amount of chest hair that took an intriguing path down firm abs before disappearing into his jeans. "Nice. Really, really nice."

She finally made eye contact but couldn't read his expression. He clutched a towel.

"You like it, so far?" he asked, moving toward her.

Who wouldn't? She needed to touch him, to flatten her hands on that perfect chest and let her fingertips seek the ridges and planes of his flesh. She could follow the thin line of hair bisecting his stomach, hook her finger on his waistband, pull him to her—

"Kincaid helped me move everything into place," he said, as if not noticing her blatant desire. "If there's something you don't like…"

It took her a moment to focus her attention on the room, not him. "I like everything I see," she said, dragging her gaze to view the freshly painted living and dining room. Some new furnishings were in place, too—end tables, two comfortable chairs to face the sofa, creating a conversation area, a sleek dining room table and chairs. "You tiled the kitchen," she said, noticing the backsplash. "It's beautiful."

"Technically Kincaid tiled. I assisted. Although it wasn't as hard as I'd anticipated."

"I love it."

"There's more. Take a look in the bedrooms." He grabbed his shirt from where it hung on a doorknob and put it on.

She felt him close behind her as she viewed the additional pieces added to the master bedroom—a chaise lounge, reading lamp and small table. Next they went into the guest room/office.

"It's starting to look like a real space," she said, moving around the room, large enough to hold a double bed and end tables.

"Your home office will be placed along that wall," Gavin said, pointing it out. "The furniture should arrive tomorrow. In the meantime, we still have boxes to unload, and more stacks of journals and folders to sort through."

"I can't believe I accumulated that much stuff."

His cell phone rang. He looked at the screen, then let it go to voice mail. Why wouldn't he answer it?

Becca had given little thought to his personal life, only his career, or lack thereof. Why had she assumed he didn't have much going on in his life?

Jealousy crept in. She hadn't felt it in so long, she didn't know how to handle it. Her fingers itched to massage his neck. And shoulders. And back. And more. "I could rub your neck for you before we go," she said. "After all, you incurred the pain in the line of duty," she added, her tongue firmly in her cheek.

"Worker's compensation?" he asked, his eyes sparkling, as if he knew exactly why she'd offered. No doubt he did. She'd practically drooled over him when she'd seen him shirtless.

"Just for a little while," he said after a few seconds. "I'm starved."

Was that his reason for limiting the time or was he worried it might lead to something else?

They went in the living room. He sat backward on one of the new chairs and rested his arms along the back, cushioning his head.

"Shirt off, please," she said, aiming for casualness.

He didn't respond right away but eventually unbuttoned it then tossed it onto the second chair. Becca got up close and set her hands on his shoulders. His skin felt warm and smooth, his muscles bunched and tight.

"Relax," she said quietly. "It'll be more effective."

She felt his shoulders relax but noticed that he wasn't shutting his eyes, his gaze aimed at the kitchen. To distract himself? Did he think he wouldn't feel her touch as much?

"Close your eyes, Gavin. Enjoy it."

"I might enjoy it too much."

Ah. So she was right. "You've done so much for me. Let me have a turn, please."

"I'm being paid for what I do."

"It's not why you're helping me all this week, and you know it."

He didn't say anything, but he did close his eyes. His whole body seemed to sink into the chair.

Becca worked his shoulders first, easing up his neck now and then but always returning to his shoulders, kneading them. When she slid her hands down his upper arms he made an involuntary sound of pleasure, so she worked his arm muscles all the way down to his wrists, taking her time, enjoying touching him and bringing him relief.

After a long while, she set her hands on his back, near his shoulder blades, and started working his back.

"Is this okay?" she asked.

"I'm mush. I couldn't stop you if I wanted to. I don't want to. You have great hands, Becca."

She should've put some music on. Or the television. The quiet accentuated her own pulse in her ears, loud and steady but escalating. He didn't stop her when she made her way down to his waist, then she realized he'd fallen asleep. She figured he'd wake up if she stopped, so she continued, not pushing hard, not kneading, but long, slow strokes meant to soothe.

A few minutes later he awakened with a start, sitting straight up. Even without seeing his face, she knew he was disoriented.

"Everything's fine," she said, more than a little pleased she'd put him to sleep.

He turned around and set his hands at her waist, drawing her close, until she had no place to go other than to straddle his lap. He kept his arms around her, keeping her from slipping.

"I fell asleep," he said.

She smiled. "Guess you needed it."

"Sleep and I haven't been friends for a while."

She did what she'd wanted to do since the moment she laid eyes on him. She ran her fingers through his hair, still slightly damp, but thick and luxurious. "I sleep like a log."

"I know. At least you don't snore."

"Thanks for the news flash." She swirled her thumbs at his temples until he closed his eyes. His hands slid down to cup her rear. After a while he began massaging her there, stroking and kneading. Aroused, she squirmed. She could feel his arousal, too.

He opened his eyes. "Stop?" he asked.

She shook her head. He shifted his legs so that she could balance more easily. Her hands on his chest, she steadied herself, anxious but waiting for him to make the moves.

"I'm at a disadvantage here," he said.

"In what way?"

"You get to touch skin."

"That really is unfair, isn't it?" She sat up a little. "I think you need to even the playing field."

As he moved from button to button, she was glad she'd put on her pretty blue bra, the one that gave her a little lift and cleavage—especially when he pressed his face into her and took a long, deep breath, as if he'd come home or something. She curved her arms up his head, her fingers burrowed in his hair as he stayed motionless, his breath hot and steady.

She'd thought he was a fairly easy-to-understand man, but this made her wonder about him, almost as if he needed her comfort more than sex—or whatever was going to come of this.

Finally he tugged her blouse off and unhooked her bra, letting the items fall to the floor. "You're perfect," he said, covering her breasts with his hands, her hard nipples pressing against his palms.

She angled toward him, wanting him to use his mouth instead. A long, low sound escaped her when he ran his thumbs over her then. She arched back, inviting more, and his warm, wet mouth settled on her nipples, his tongue exploring her leisurely, thoroughly, his teeth scraping her lightly.

Her fantasy man was proving himself real. And she wanted him…

Then the doorbell rang.

Chapter Eight

"Special delivery," a woman called through the door. Not just any woman. Shana.

Gavin helped Becca stand, then he scooped up her bra and blouse, shoved them into her hands, and she took off for her bedroom. He put on his own shirt as he went to the door, finger combing his hair before he opened it.

Shana looked ready to greet him then tried to sneak a glance into the room, a view he was blocking. "Did I interrupt something?" Her eyes sparkled.

"Yes." He reached for the large plastic-wrapped bundle she carried. "We were moving furniture. Come in."

"I called you a while ago, but you didn't pick up

the phone. I figured I'd take a chance that one of you was home, so I didn't have to haul this—" She stopped in her tracks, plunked her fists on her hips. "No way. You did not get this room painted—" she moved toward the kitchen "—*and* the tile done today by yourself. *No way.*"

"O ye of little faith."

She laughed. "Who'd you hire?"

He stuffed his hands in his pockets. "Kincaid."

Her mouth dropped open. "You owe me a tune-up."

"I do."

"You didn't play fair at all."

"What do you care? You won."

She clamped her mouth shut at that and then pointed a finger at him. "You planned this. I don't need charity, Gavin."

"What charity? I didn't realize how over my head I was until after you left. The work had to get done somehow. Kincaid was the first person who came to mind. So, take your car into Mather's and have Ed send me the bill. And for the record, Shana? I did participate. I painted, and I helped tile. Life skills, Kincaid called them. He made me work right alongside him."

"Bully for him."

"You weren't supposed to be here until Friday," he said to his sister, accusation in his voice that he couldn't control. She'd interrupted his moment with Becca at the worst possible time.

Or the best, his mind whispered. Making love with her wasn't a good idea, and he knew it.

Becca came out of the bedroom then, looking pulled together. But his brain was burned with an image of her without her blouse, how beautiful she was, her slender frame, smooth skin and amazing breasts.

He'd also fallen asleep during her massage. A short, deep, satisfying sleep.

"Hi, Shana," Becca said, seeming a little hesitant to step into the fray. She'd probably heard every word. "I can't believe how transformed this place is already, and Gavin says you're not done yet."

"Not even close. Hi, yourself." Shana smiled. "I found the perfect light fixture for over your dining-room table while I was at lunch today. Want to see it?"

"Absolutely." Becca put a hand on Shana's arm. "Have you eaten? We hadn't decided whether to go out or have something delivered. We'd love to have you join us."

We would? Gavin thought as he cut away the plastic from the light. Actually he thought it was one of the worst ideas ever. Becca could learn way too much about him, things he wasn't ready to share, if he ever was. Four more days and their relationship would end.

"I appreciate the invitation," Shana said. "But I want to get home to my little girl. Another time? Maybe on a weekend?"

"It's a date. Oh! The fixture is gorgeous."

The white-glass-and-nickel pendant light was perfect, Gavin thought. Shana really did have the eye. "Good choice," he said.

"I'll install it on Friday. Unless you'd like to make another bet with me, big brother." Her expression held challenge and humor.

"Wouldn't even attempt it. How do you know how?"

"It's a life skill."

Gavin laughed.

"Anyway, I only have to replace the other fixture. I couldn't have wired the space. I leave that for the pros."

"I absolutely love it and everything else you've chosen," Becca said. "Including the paint color. Do you have any business cards I could hand out? I would highly recommend you."

Shana gave Gavin a look, as if she was surprised but trying hard not to show it in front of her client.

"I don't have any with me," Shana said, "but I'll bring some to you. Thank you, Becca." She hugged Becca and then Gavin, whispering in his ear, "You're a good brother."

He smiled as she left, her praise warming him.

"So," Becca said, slipping her hands in her pockets. "It's probably not a good idea for us to pick up where we left off."

"Oh, it would be a good idea, all right, but probably not a wise one," he said, knowing she was right and sorry that she was. And she somehow managed to look relieved and disappointed at the same time. "Want to hit the Thai restaurant?"

"That'd be good."

He waited while she got her purse, his gaze lingering on the chair of pleasure, as he would think of it from now on. Becca had great hands, strong yet soothing. The fact he'd fallen asleep told him that even his subconscious trusted her. He wondered if spending the whole night in her bed would let him sleep better.

"Are you okay?" Becca asked, suddenly standing right in front of him, frowning.

No one had worried about him in a long time, probably because he didn't generally let anyone that close. The concerned look on Becca's face would usually be a good enough reason for him to back off, but he gathered her close and held her tight. "Everything is good," he said, meaning it.

A minute later they were on their way to dinner. Then they spent the remainder of the evening unboxing, sorting, putting away and tossing. The file cabinets would be delivered in the morning, then all the paperwork could be tucked away, out of sight.

Her house would be a home finally. And he would be irrelevant—unless she decided to let the lie continue with her brothers instead of telling the truth.

When she yawned he checked the time. Almost midnight. He was used to running on empty, but she wasn't.

I accept your offer!

Please send me two free
Harlequin® Special Edition®
novels and two mystery
gifts (gifts worth about $10).
I understand that these books
are completely free—even
the shipping and handling will
be paid—and I am under no
obligation to purchase anything, ever,
as explained on the back of this card.

About how many NEW paperback fiction books have you purchased in the past 3 months?

❏ 0-2   ❏ 3-6   ❏ 7 or more
FDEV   **FDE7**   **FDFK**

235/335 HDL

Please Print

FIRST NAME

LAST NAME

ADDRESS

APT.#   CITY

STATE/PROV.   ZIP/POSTAL CODE

Visit us online at
www.ReaderService.com

The Reader Service—Here's how it works: Accepting your 2 free books and 2 free gifts (gifts valued at approximately $10.00) places you under no obligation to buy anything. You may keep the books and gifts and return the shipping statement marked "cancel". If you do not cancel, about a month later we'll send you 6 additional books and bill you just $4.24 each in the U.S. or $4.99 each in Canada. That is a savings of 15% off the cover price. It's quite a bargain! Shipping and handling is just 50¢ per book in the U.S. or 75¢ per book in Canada.* You may cancel at any time, but if you choose to continue, every month we'll send you 6 more books, which you may either purchase at the discount price or return to us and cancel your subscription.

*Terms and prices subject to change without notice. Prices do not include applicable taxes. Sales tax applicable in N.Y. Canadian residents will be charged applicable taxes. Offer not valid in Quebec. Credit or debit balances in a customer's account(s) may be offset by any other outstanding balance owed by or to the customer. Please allow 4 to 6 weeks for delivery. Offer available while quantities last. All orders subject to credit approval. Books received may not be as shown.

▼ If offer card is missing write to: The Reader Service, P.O. Box 1867, Buffalo, NY 14240-1867 or visit www.ReaderService.com ▼

NO POSTAGE
NECESSARY
IF MAILED
IN THE
UNITED STATES

BUSINESS REPLY MAIL
FIRST-CLASS MAIL   PERMIT NO. 717   BUFFALO, NY

POSTAGE WILL BE PAID BY ADDRESSEE

THE READER SERVICE

PO BOX 1867

BUFFALO NY 14240-9952

"You must be wiped out," he said. She was sitting cross-legged in the office, a few piles of paper spread out in front of her. "I hadn't realized how late it was."

She smiled sleepily, which he found incredibly sexy. Then when she stretched, his mouth went dry.

"The end is in sight," she said, grabbing hold of his outstretched hand and standing.

"How're things going at work with Chip? Is he speaking to you yet?"

"He's been distant. People have noticed." She shrugged. "That, too, shall end."

"Have you decided what you're going to tell your brothers?"

"Yes. Then no." She shrugged. "I usually make up my mind quickly. If I had less time to think about it, I'd probably do better. Does that make sense?"

"It does." He smoothed her hair, which had gotten appealingly messy over the course of the evening, and then he kissed her forehead.

She leaned into him for a minute. "My knight," she said. "Rescuing me from myself."

"I'm glad I don't have a trusty steed to feed."

"Instead you have a mighty sports car that you probably have to feed with gas every two hundred miles."

"Two hundred and fifty."

"I stand corrected." She pushed away, although she seemed reluctant. "I know it seems like I'm always thanking you, Gavin, but you're always deserving it."

He should be thanking *her* for giving him something important to do to keep his mind busy, for making him feel needed. "Oh, yeah, it's been such a hardship spending time with you."

Her smile lit up the room. He liked this sleepy, sexy Becca. "Will you sleep in a little tomorrow?" he asked.

"I doubt it. I'm programmed for six-thirty."

"Okay. I'll see you for breakfast at seven."

She followed him to the front door. "You don't have to come so early, you know. Sleep in."

"I might." But he wouldn't. He just didn't want to argue the point.

He opened the door, turned around, took a last look at her. She raised her brows in question. "Have you ever been in love?" he asked.

She blinked in surprise to the intrusive question, but she answered. "I thought I was once. I was nineteen. What does anyone really know at nineteen? Have you? Been in love?"

"No. Have you ever lived with a man?"

"I shared a house with two guys and another girl in college. We didn't…commingle."

"Commingle," he repeated, amused. "Interesting word choice."

She shrugged. "How about you?"

"No."

"Why not?"

It was a strange conversation to be having in her doorway, after midnight, in the middle of the workweek. The whole building seemed to be sleeping. "Never wanted to."

"Not even tempted?" she asked.

"Not even. You?"

"Once."

"The guy you thought you loved?"

She nodded. "We would've probably killed each other."

He laughed at the outrageous idea. She grinned back.

"Sleep well, Becca."

"You, too. Don't forget to take off your armor before you get in bed, Sir Gavin. You might not be able to get up." She winked at him, then shut the door.

He was glad she did, because he couldn't seem to make himself leave. Ever since he'd started wondering if sleeping with her would help him get some rest, he hadn't been able to think of much else. Would having her there to hold on to help?

Gavin was tempted to go back and knock on her door, ask if he could stay. Instead he punched the down button for the elevator and then made his way back to his hotel. He got ready for bed, leaving his drapes open, as always, lying on his side to look out into the night. This evening there were clouds that hid the stars. The metallic smell of impending rain had assaulted him as he left her place. Rain would be good, he thought. Clean things up a bit. Start the day fresh.

Start fresh. Maybe that's what he needed for himself. Maybe going back to work in a week or two wasn't the answer. He certainly wasn't ready yet. His hands wouldn't be steady, he would question every decision he made. And the longer he stayed away, the less he wanted to return to his practice. To that life.

He couldn't delay his decision forever, he knew that. But it could wait until he'd helped Becca through this weekend. He kept his commitments.

But once the weekend was over, he would make his choices.

Chapter Nine

"You're sure?" Gavin asked.

"If you think we can pull it off, then, yes." Becca paced her living room, not paying attention to how beautiful it looked. It was Saturday morning. Shana had finished up the decorating last night. Becca had cried, it looked so nice.

"Do you think we can, Gavin?" Her worry about her brothers' arrival was becoming increasingly stronger.

"I don't see why not." He didn't look quite as confident as he sounded.

"I think they'll expect me to be behaving a little differently," she said. "After all, I've never been married before."

"You're probably right."

She pressed her hands to her stomach. Gavin had made her eat some toast, which had helped settle her queasiness some but not completely.

"C'mere," he said, taking her hand, leading her to the couch and forcing her to sit beside him. "Let's run through this one last time. Why did you pretend you eloped in the first place?"

She focused on the goal. "For them, especially Eric. He won't relax until he knows I'm being taken care of. Only then will he give up his constant sense of responsibility to me and my happiness and let himself find his own."

"It's a very good reason, right?"

"Right." The tightness inside her eased a bit. "I know my reasoning was good, even though my solution may be over the top. I'm not sure I can fake the lie for twenty-four hours. I could never pull a fast one on Eric. Or Jeff, for that matter. He's only two years older, so we spent a lot more time together than I did with Sam and Trent."

"I'll be beside you every minute, Becca. You won't have to handle it alone."

"You're really okay with doing this?"

"I've thought about it for nine days. The more I've come to know you, the easier the idea has become." He squeezed her hand. "But if at any time you decide you want to come clean, I'll be here for you, too."

Every day he became more of a gift to her, Becca thought. And every day she fell for him a little more.

She didn't want to fall in love with him. Refused to. What a horrible situation *that* would create.

"Okay. Game on," she said firmly, looking at Gavin. "That was good thinking, bringing some of your clothes to hang in my closet and your stuff for the bathroom." Not to mention, he'd put copies of *Sports Illustrated* and *Car and Driver* on the coffee table. Extra beer in the refrigerator. Plenty of food for men with big appetites to snack on. Gavin had taken care of every detail.

Becca glanced at the clock on her mantel. Half hour to go. Thirty nerve-racking minutes…

Gavin got up from the couch and went to Becca's iPod dock, deciding she needed something else to occupy herself until her family arrived. He scrolled through her music list, chose a tune, started it, then asked her to dance. He hoped she wouldn't beg off.

He needn't have worried. She grabbed his hand, bounced right up and got caught up in the rhythm. She danced well, moved gracefully, put her whole body into it. As did he. He loved to dance, had always found a freedom in it. When the song stopped and another started, it was slower, and he pulled her into his arms and made good use of the open space near the front door. They were a good match, perfectly attuned to each other's bodies, anticipating well, rarely making a misstep.

It was a rare thing to find, that kind of matchup.

They danced without talking, smiling the whole

time, the music changing from fast to slow to fast again. He whirled her in circles. She danced around him as if he were a maypole. He hadn't seen this playful side of her, and he liked it. A whole lot.

She looked relaxed and carefree, an expression that didn't fade, not even when her doorbell rang. She danced to the door and flung it open, revealing a blockade of four men, all of whom looked athletic and blood related.

Becca squealed like a teenager then hugged each of them, her happiness contagious. No one could stay serious around her. Her eyes sparkled brightly as she introduced everyone to Gavin.

"Callahan?" Jeff repeated upon finally being told Gavin's last name, then grinned. "Another good Irish name."

Gavin already knew who was who from their photographs, but he could've picked out Eric regardless. They all had hair in varying shades of brown, but Eric's was graying at the temples, giving him a patriarchal look—along with the fact his handshake was not just firm but hard, and his gaze unflinching, although it softened a little when Becca came up beside Gavin and slipped her arm around his waist then leaned against him. Her cheeks were still flushed from the dancing.

And she didn't look nervous at all. She looked happy, deep down, sincerely happy. He slipped his arm around her shoulders.

"Were you playing handball or something when we got here?" Eric asked.

"Dancing," Becca answered.

"Whoa, sis!" Jeff said. "Your place looks awesome. Doc has obviously been a good influence."

"There's even food in the fridge," she said, not taking offense. "Beer, too."

"Are you hungry?" Gavin asked. "We've got plenty of sandwich stuff."

A chorus of "sounds good" followed. Then the group moved toward the kitchen, although one brother—Sam—went to stand at the window to look at the view.

A great deal of commotion ensued, playful pushing and shoving and elbow jabbing amongst Trent, Jeff and Becca, who put herself in the middle of the fray, her happiness not diminishing a bit, nerves not showing.

"So, you're a doctor," Eric said to Gavin as they leaned against the counter, watching the byplay.

"Yes." He became aware of all the brothers at least partially focusing their attention on the conversation—which meant worry started to settle in Becca's eyes. "Ob-gyn."

"Do you like it?" Jeff asked, his eyes twinkling.

"I do."

"Are you good at it?" Eric asked.

"I am."

Eric gave him a long look, then nodded, as if he liked the short, direct answers.

"How about you?" Gavin asked.

"I've got my hands in a few different ventures," he said with a shrug.

"But he's also a math professor. He's kind of a Jekyll and Hyde," Jeff said.

Eric smiled tolerantly at his brother. "I've been thinking about moving to Sacramento," Eric said after a brief pause.

The blood drained from Becca's face. Gavin's first instinct was to go to her, but she rallied herself quickly enough to look happy about the news. Maybe she was. Maybe she would make the decision to tell Eric the truth now. Get it over with.

"Are you serious?" she asked.

"Very. Would that please you?"

Quiet settled in the space, as if everyone was holding their breath. "I'd love it if *all* of you moved here!"

Sam walked away from the window to join them. "I've been considering it, as well," he said coolly, calmly, keeping his gaze on Becca.

"Me, too," Trent said, looking up from building his sandwich, winking at his sister.

Jeff grinned. "Well, hell. I don't want to be left out."

Becca's expression morphed from shock to joy to confusion. She pressed a hand to her stomach, indicating turmoil, then the conversation turned noisy again, all the brothers except Eric contributing to it.

Gavin considered pulling today's classified ads from the recycling bin, then realized he didn't know what they did for a living. They could all be in jobs or professions not usually advertised in the newspaper. Plus, they weren't really his brothers-in-law, so it was none of his business.

A concept that hadn't stopped Becca. She'd left a copy of the paper on the counter this morning where he couldn't miss it, opened to the classifieds.

He didn't figure it was by accident, since she wasn't a subscriber, traveling as much as she did. So she must have bought a copy specifically for him.

At first he'd been annoyed. She'd hinted now and then about him finding permanent work, talked endlessly about her satisfaction with her job, her sense of accomplishment and pride. He couldn't tell her he already had a job because he wasn't ready to talk to her—or anyone—about it yet. He had a feeling, however, that Eric would find out, now that he knew Gavin's last name, and that cat would be out of the bag.

He and Becca were both treading in dangerous waters.

The Sheridans spent the afternoon reminiscing, this being the first time in years all five of them had been together at the same time. The teasing was lighthearted, the stories of Becca as a child told with brotherly love and enthusiasm. She was obviously the adored little sister. Eric didn't say much, as if still assessing Gavin and finding him lacking. At dinnertime they walked to a nearby restaurant, lingered over a nice meal, toasted several times to Becca and Gavin's happiness and a long, fruitful marriage.

The three younger brothers asked about finding a nightclub with live music and dancing so they could check out the Sacramento scene, to see if it was worth making the move. Gavin was fine with going to a loud club where talking wouldn't even be possible, but by the time they got to the club, Eric wasn't feeling well.

Planning on checking out my doctoring skills? Gavin asked the man silently. "Something you ate?" he asked aloud.

"I don't know." His face was a little pale. He couldn't fake that.

"Gavin and I will go back to the loft with you," Becca said, concern in her eyes. "You three can head to the club. We'll see you in the morning."

"Want us to swing by and get you when we're done?" Sam asked Eric.

"I'm sure I can get to the hotel on my own. I'll see you later."

Gavin figured Eric wanted to be alone with him and Becca, to ask whatever questions were on his mind, but whatever they were, he didn't get a chance to ask. He headed straight for the guest bathroom.

"Food poisoning, do you think?" Becca asked Gavin as they sat on the couch, waiting.

"Hard to say." He wrapped a hand around both of hers, tucked in her lap. "You've held up well."

Her smile was a little lopsided. "Some close calls."

"You were right. Eric can be intimidating."

"He's been watching you like a hawk," she said.

"I know. Do you think I'm passing inspection?"

"Your guess is as good as mine. I'm assuming he'll take me aside for a heart-to-heart before they leave tomorrow."

"Me, too," Gavin said, sure of it. "I like them, Becca. They're all great." And because he liked them, he felt even worse about the deceit. "I've also picked up on how protective they are of you."

"They've toned it down, big-time." She leaned into him, keeping her voice low. "Thank you again for making this place a real home. You heard the amazement in their voices when I took them on a tour of the rooms. You, rightfully, got the credit."

He kissed her hair. "Apparently I've been a good influence."

She nestled closer. "Obviously I needed it."

He wasn't going to want to leave tomorrow. The thought had been swirling in his head all day. The job would be done, but he...wasn't.

"Any chance you've got an extra toothbrush?" Eric asked from behind them. He was leaning against the bathroom doorjamb. His face had gone even paler, his skin looked clammy.

"Of course." Becca hopped up and hurried off to her bedroom.

Gavin went to stand by Eric. "What do you think it

is? We had the same thing for dinner, and I feel fine. Lunch, too, for that matter. Have you been around someone with the flu?"

Eric shook his head. "I didn't feel great this morning. I've had a headache since I got up. I hate to ask this of you, but I don't think I can make it to the hotel." He aimed his next question at Becca as she returned and handed him the item he'd requested. "Do you mind if I bunk here?"

Becca looked at Gavin, whose expression gave away nothing. "Of course we don't mind. What else do you need?"

"If you would call Sam and let him know?"

"Sure." Becca put a hand on his forehead. "You feel cold."

"Do you have a thermometer?" Gavin asked her.

"I'm sorry, no."

"I thought doctors always had a medical bag with them with emergency supplies in it," Eric said.

"Some do. Aside from the headache, are you in pain?"

"No pain. Just feel like crap."

Leaving them to talk, Becca headed into the guest room to turn down the bedding. Two thoughts held court in her head—her big, strong brother was ill, and Gavin was going to have to stay the night. In her bedroom.

"Don't fuss," Eric said, coming into the room.

"It's my right as your sister." She couldn't bear

seeing him sick, couldn't remember a time when he had been. He always seemed invincible.

"I'm sure I'll be fine by morning."

"Well, don't play macho man. If you need anything, knock on my—our door."

Gavin came in carrying a small bucket. "Just in case," he said, setting it next to the bed. "I put a glass in the bathroom. Keep yourself hydrated if you feel you can keep it down."

"Thanks. Now good night, both of you."

"If you get worse, or develop any pain, wake me up," Gavin said then shut the door behind him.

Sam didn't answer his phone, so Becca left a voice mail. After that there was nothing to do except face facts—they had a long night ahead of them. They'd acknowledged their attraction to each other. They'd kissed a couple of times. They'd had that moment in her living room, half-naked, all heat. They'd barely gotten started exploring each other when Shana had arrived unexpectedly. They'd been careful since then not to put themselves in temptation's way.

Now they had no choice. Could they resist?

Did they have to?

"Do you want anything from the kitchen?" Gavin asked, heading there.

"I'm still full from dinner," she said, following him, wondering how he could possibly eat, then saw him take the water pitcher from the refrigerator and pour himself a glass. "Well," she said. "It looks like we've got a situation."

"Yes, we do."

"I'll sleep on the chaise," she said. *Change my mind, Gavin. Change my mind.*

He took a long drink of his water and then set the glass down, looking at it for several seconds before finally answering her, his gaze intense. "Okay."

Okay? *O-kay?* That was all he had to say on the matter? "I'm going to take a shower," she said then turned and walked away.

"I'm going to stay out here for a while, in case Eric needs something."

She almost groaned. She'd forgotten her brother instantly and completely in her desire to sleep with Gavin. They couldn't have sex with her brother right next door. Of course they couldn't. No wonder Gavin had given her such a look. He probably thought she'd lost her mind.

Maybe she had. Maybe all the stress of the past couple of weeks had smashed her common sense, usually so reliable, into smithereens.

Becca took a quick shower, then dressed in flannel pajama bottoms and a tank top. She slipped a robe on before she went into the living room to say she was done. As she padded down the hall she realized the lights were out except for a night-light he'd plugged in between the guest room and bathroom, in case Eric got up.

Gavin's thoughtfulness, his foresight, should've stopped surprising her, but it never did. He'd anticipated her needs since the first time he'd come to her loft. He'd been giving her a lot more than she'd given him in return. In fact, she'd been emotional and frazzled and not at all herself. Yet he'd been unceasingly kind, patient and tolerant. He'd made her relax, sit back, put up her feet. He'd fixed her meals, taken her for walks, made her laugh.

Danced with her.

Lied for her.

She spotted him on her balcony, bathed in moonlight, his arms resting on the rail, looking into the distance. As she approached him he stood and scrubbed his face with both hands. The unguarded moment, seeming to signal frustration, caught her off guard. Had he merely been playing a role for her? Was he exhausted and ready to finish the job?

Had she asked too much of him?

She joined him on the balcony. He turned toward her but didn't touch her.

"I've decided to sleep on the couch," he said.

"You can't do that. What would Eric think?"

"If he catches me, I'll tell him I wanted to be close by."

"Like being in the room next door is all that far?" she asked before she could censor herself. She had no right to demand anything of him, and he was presenting a good solution.

Because she ached to touch him, she crossed her arms. "I'm sorry. That was unfair. You've done so much for me. I'm very grateful."

"Everything I've done was because I wanted

to, Becca. Chose to. But the lie got harder when I met and liked your brothers. I don't know what I expected, based on what you told me. All I know is they're great. All of them. I envy your closeness."

"You seem close with Shana."

"We're getting there. Things have always been okay with Dixie, too. But we didn't have that bond that you all have. Your parents must have been something special."

"I wish I remembered them better," she whispered, saying out loud what had haunted her for years. "I was thirteen, old enough to have memories, but I can't recall very much. A lot of what I remember is what my brothers talk about, or photographs or the few videos we have." Tears welled. Her throat burned. "I feel so cheated. I miss my parents so much."

Gavin's arms came around her, comforting and soothing until she stopped crying.

"If your brothers move here," he said, "you'll have family close again."

"I'm not sure that's entirely a good thing." Of course it was, but not until she'd gotten herself out of the jam she'd gotten into by making up a husband.

"Do you think they're serious? I got the sense Eric was throwing the idea out there to test our reaction, and then the rest of them went along with it."

"You could be right." She pushed away, swiped her fingers across her cheeks. "I'm tired."

"Me, too. I need a shower first."

"That's fine. Good thing you brought your stuff with you."

A couple of minutes later Becca was in bed listening to her shower run. She'd left a small lamp on by her bedside, had set a blanket and pillow on the foot of the bed that he could carry into the living room.

She pictured him, water pouring over his body. She wished she could magically transport herself into the shower with him. She would take her time soaping his skin, gliding her hands along him...

The water shut off. Becca fanned herself with her covers, creating a cooling breeze over her overheated body. After a few minutes the bathroom door opened. He wore a T-shirt and maybe sweatpants. It was hard to tell from where she was.

He spotted the blanket and pillow, grabbed them and walked to the door. "Good night, Becca."

She got to her knees just as he opened the door. "Please don't go," she whispered.

He stopped, was silhouetted in the doorway.

She got out of bed, came up behind him, put her hands on his back, felt his muscles bunch. "Stay with me."

Then she waited for what seemed like an eternity for his answer.

Chapter Ten

Gavin's head filled with reasons why he shouldn't stay, all of them good. Her brother was in the apartment. The job would end tomorrow afternoon, so why muddy the waters now? He still had some healing to do and decisions to make. His home was in San Francisco. So was his work.

Those were short-term reasons. There were some long-term ones, too. The fact that Becca was enmeshed in her own career as cofounder of a thriving business. It wasn't a job she could telecommute from easily, if at all. She worked long hours, as he'd always done. She even was on the road a lot.

Of course, they didn't have to look at the big picture. They *could* just have sex without expectations of a future relationship, especially since she was never going to marry and eventually he wanted to. He wanted a wife and children. Balance in his life. A future. But he wasn't ready for that yet, either.

"I can hear you thinking," she said, pressing her lips to his back, giving him chills. "It doesn't need to be so difficult, Gavin."

He heard her voice quaver, proof it was difficult for her, not just him. And it must have cost her a lot to be the instigator, since whoever made the first move ran the greatest risk for rejection.

He admired her for that, but he couldn't let it get in the way of his decision. Because he hadn't even factored in his biggest concern—nights were the worst for him, when all his doubts shouted in his head. When his visions of a mother and child turned vivid. Becca had only seen him in control. He didn't want her left with a different impression of him, especially now that they were near the end of their time together.

"If all we're going to do is act on our attraction," he said, shutting the door so they wouldn't be overheard, "then we could just as easily wait until tomorrow, when we're alone."

"If we wait until tomorrow, you'll find a reason to change your mind. Something logical and sensible."

She was right. He would do that. Or maybe she would.

But was that a good enough reason to take this

big step now? That was something the old Gavin would've done, not the man he'd been working toward becoming.

He closed his eyes for a moment, focusing on his sometimes terrifying nights. "It's not a good idea, Becca." He left the room, her disappointment palpable. Or maybe it was his disappointment, which was why he felt it so strongly.

Her couch was comfortable, but he still tossed and turned. After a while he heard the guest-room door open and Eric pad next door to the bathroom.

"Are you okay?" Gavin asked when Eric emerged.

"I'm better." He walked to the sofa. "What're you doing out here?"

"I wanted to be nearby. Just in case."

"I'm going to survive. I'm sure you'd much rather be sleeping with your wife." He'd almost phrased it as a question. There was a bit of a lilt to the word *wife,* as if challenging Gavin, not just commenting.

"If you're sure," Gavin said.

"My stomach has settled down." Still he waited.

Making sure Gavin left? He had no choice but to go to Becca's room. He scooped up the pillow and blanket. "See you in the morning."

"Right," Eric said.

Was that humor in his voice? Eric couldn't know the truth, yet he seemed to be getting a kick out of the moment for some reason.

Gavin opened Becca's door quietly. He tiptoed past her bed, heading to the chaise.

"What's going on?" she asked, turning on the small light on her nightstand.

"Eric's feeling better." He tossed his pillow onto his new temporary bed. "He ordered me to sleep with my wife."

"That chaise is way too small for you." She stood. "You take the bed."

He could've spent the next ten minutes arguing with her, but he knew it would be useless. She would have her way. "Thanks," he said as they met in the middle.

She didn't say anything, but her eyes met his, and that was all it took. To hell with sleep. He could catch up tomorrow night.

"Stay," he said, the words coming out low and harsh, or maybe desperate. "Sleep with me."

"Just sleep?" she asked, laying a hand on his abdomen.

"Eventually."

"Gavin," she whispered just before he slipped his arms around her and kissed her.

It was the first kiss they'd shared with the intention of taking it further, so it was...different. Freer, bolder, more daring. Her lips melded with his, her mouth transferred heat and desire. Soft, sexy sounds vibrated along her throat, flattering and arousing. She slipped her hands under his T-shirt, her fingers like fiery tentacles, leaving warmth behind even after she moved on. She shoved his shirt up his body, over his head, but before she could touch him, he peeled her tank top over her head and hurled it across the room.

"I was so irritated with Shana for interrupting us the other night," he said, cupping her breasts, circling her nipples with his thumbs, fulfilling the fantasy barely begun days ago and relived every night since as he lay in bed watching the stars.

"I figured you were relieved," Becca said, her voice hitching when he traded his mouth for his hands.

"I tried to tell myself that." He nibbled her hard flesh until she groaned. She tasted of lavender soap, sweet and feminine. "How about you?"

"I didn't bother to lie to myself. Oh, don't stop." She arched her back as he dragged his tongue down her stomach, tugging her pajama bottoms off as he went, exposing her beautiful body to his eyes and hands. Her pajamas pooled at her feet. He ran his fingers down her legs, lifted each foot free, nudged her toward the bed until she came up against it and landed with a bounce.

She hooked her fingers in his sweatpants and lowered them. He took over when she couldn't reach to push them all the way down, then they were naked and totally exposed. *Appreciated.* She was looking up at him, but her hands were busy elsewhere, exploring and teasing.

"The first night you came here," she said, "I thought you looked like a sculpture of the world's most perfect male. And that was with your clothes on." She lowered her gaze, provoking an explosive reaction in him that threatened to end things before they started. "Now I see that *perfect* is too bland a word."

He grabbed her wrists, moved her hands out of the way, then started returning the favor to her, as slowly and gently as he could, even though he was shaking from holding back. He touched her, tasted her. Savored her.

"I'm on the pill," she said.

Her words made him hesitate. He never forgot birth control. Never. Until now...

Then he stopped thinking and simply enjoyed, moving her so her feet weren't dangling off the bed, blanketing her body with his. She opened up to him while at the same time pulled him closer, saying his name, broadcasting her need. She rose to capture his lips urgently, desperately. He inched inside her, was welcomed by her tight, wet warmth. She grabbed hold of his hair as she raised and lowered her hips in rhythm with his. He tried to wait for her, but he couldn't. Not one second longer.

Luckily neither could she. He kissed her, muffling their sounds as they hit the peak at the same time, stayed there for an eternity then ever so slowly came back to earth.

Awareness took longer. The most he could manage was to roll onto his side, taking her with him, their legs entwined, their bodies almost adhering. She tightened her arms when he would've moved back just enough to look at her. He felt her breath, hot and shaky, against his throat. Her shower-fresh fragrance mingled with the scent of sex, a heady combination, one that had him already wanting a second round.

She felt good in his arms. Perfect.

He tried again to pull back. Once again Becca clasped him, not letting him move.

"I'm not going anywhere," he said.

Becca didn't want him to look at her, to see the love she felt, was overwhelmed with, reflected in her eyes. In a few more minutes she could hide it, from herself, too. But right now he would see. Considering how he'd fought making love with her, she knew he didn't feel the same.

And she had no business feeling it at all. It couldn't lead anywhere. There were far too many barriers. He wanted a wife and children....

Somehow she needed to let him know that everything was fine, that she wouldn't demand from him what he couldn't give.

She just didn't know how to go about it. Things like that didn't happen, not to her, anyway.

But she wanted very much to simply enjoy it, especially the way he stroked her hair, then let his hands glide down her back and over her rear then back up again, exploring as he went. Teasing.

"Are you okay?" he asked into her hair, his voice a little obscured.

"I'm quite satisfied, thank you."

He laughed, which relaxed her enough to angle back and look at him. "How about you?"

"I'll see your *satisfied* and raise you two *gratifieds*."

"I'm all in," she said, smiling, glad he was keeping the tone light, as if they'd just played a hand of poker.

"That's my line." He ran a finger across her lips. "I was definitely all in."

"Yes, you were. A perfect fit, too." She dragged a hand down his chest, his stomach, his abdomen, then beyond. "Not much recovery time for you."

He shook his head slowly, a knowing smile on his face, one that made her feel sexy enough to take charge. She shoved him onto his back then straddled him, enjoying the admiration in his eyes. With his help, she took him inside her.

"All in," she murmured, closing her eyes and letting herself just feel him. Suddenly he jackknifed up and his mouth was on her breast. She wrapped her legs around his back, her arms around his head and held him there, lost in the pleasure. "I'd guessed you'd be like this," she said, her words raspy.

"Like what?"

"Adventurous."

He lifted his head. "You must have led a sheltered life."

"Is that a complaint?"

"Hardly."

Amazingly she hadn't felt a moment's shyness around him, or worry that she might say or do something he wouldn't like. She'd felt an instant openness with him that was thrilling but also comfortable. The fact she could feel both at the same time came as a surprise, as did her quick, spiraling arousal in the position they were in. Caught off guard by her swift ascent to climax, she gasped. Then when he slid a hand between their bodies, intensifying her reaction, she groaned.

"Shh," Gavin said, covering her mouth with his, aware that they weren't alone in the quiet loft.

"Sorry," she panted, "but—"

"I know. Go with it. Just go quietly." He devoured her mouth as she peaked, a powerful reaction that sped up his own electrifying response, even better than the first time. Longer, more powerful. More satisfying.

She went limp, her arms draped over his shoulders, her face pressed into his neck. He wanted to tell her what it meant to him, how he hadn't felt this alive in so long. So very long. But either she'd fallen asleep against him or she was too relaxed and content to talk. She made sleepy sounds of satisfaction, but that seemed all she was capable of. He understood that.

Gavin maneuvered her onto her side and tucked himself behind her.

"Mmm," she murmured, wriggling closer. "That was really, really nice."

He laughed softly at the understatement. "I agree."

"If I wake you in the middle of the night for another go-round, would that be okay?" she asked, sounding sleepier and sleepier.

The mere idea of it gave him something to look forward to. "I might be able to squeeze you in."

Her laugh faded into slow, even breaths. She was out.

A few hours later, true to her word, she began caressing him as he pretended to be asleep. He didn't pretend for long. He didn't want to waste any time. After all, their idyll couldn't last. In a few hours they would face her brothers again.

They would've had time to do a little background check on him—at least, *he* would, if it were his sister.

Or Becca might decide to come clean with them.

Anything could happen.

Anticipation surged through him. It wasn't the way he'd figured he would return to the land of the living, but he'd take what he could get.

Chapter Eleven

Breakfast was a noisy affair. Sam, Trent and Jeff recounted stories of their club hopping, declaring Sacramento's nightlife "okay" and the women "above average." Faint praise, Gavin thought. He wondered how serious they were about moving to Sacramento.

Most of all he wondered about Eric, who ate a couple of pieces of French toast, but skipped the rest, although he said he felt better, but didn't look it.

Becca had put herself in the middle of the familial circle, looking happily beleaguered by her teasing brothers, but catching Gavin's eye now and then, smiling in an all-knowing way.

It'd been a hell of a night.

He hadn't slept, hadn't cared about it, either, taking comfort in holding her, listening to her sleep, finding satisfaction in making love at three o'clock in the morning. He'd forgotten how leisurely middle-of-the-night sex could be, those slow, rolling climaxes that weren't always as strong but lasted pleasurably longer.

At some point today, he would probably crash, but not before they talked about what came next, a discussion they'd decided to put off until they were alone.

Considering how much could change between now and then, they'd been wise to delay, he thought. They needed to be flexible, to adapt and adjust in a heartbeat.

And apparently that heartbeat was about to happen. He watched Eric approach him in the kitchen where he was stacking the dishes in the sink. Eric had a look in his eye, one that said he meant business.

"Let's go for a walk," Eric said.

"Okay." He stopped at the dining-room table, where Becca and her other brothers were lingering over coffee. "Eric and I are taking a walk," he said, bending to kiss her, feeling her surprise. "Are we telling the truth?" he whispered.

"Only if you feel backed into a corner," she whispered back, then kissed him, looking like a happy wife. "Be nice," she ordered Eric.

He gave her a look that said this was between the

two men and that she should stay out of it. Gavin grabbed his jacket then met Eric at the front door.

"How long do you think you'll be?" Becca asked, having moved to stand next to Eric, not able to hide the worry in her voice.

"As long as it takes," Eric answered.

"It's fine," Gavin said to her, rubbing her arm. "Use the time to see how serious those three are about moving here now that they've checked out some of the single women in town." He opened the door, letting Eric precede him, who then made him wait until they'd left the building and started walking before he opened the discussion. This was the first Sunday morning Gavin had spent in downtown Sacramento. There was traffic, but it was mild, as was the weather.

"I had a background check done on you overnight," Eric said.

"That doesn't surprise me." In fact, he'd wondered why Becca hadn't done the same thing, but apparently she hadn't or she would've had questions. Big questions.

"I would've done it sooner," Eric said, "but I didn't know your last name. She always referred to you as Doc."

An accusatory tone coated his words. Apparently the blame was Gavin's. "We never talked about it. I didn't know she was keeping you in the dark, Eric. She must've had her reasons."

"I can't imagine what they would be. You're well

established in a thriving ob-gyn practice with three other doctors. She should be happy to share that information."

And now Becca's brother knew something that she didn't. How was this going to play out? How many lies did he have to tell? "Maybe she wanted to surprise you. Let us meet first."

They rounded a corner, their strides getting longer and faster as emotions were added to the mix.

"Surprise me? Yes, I've found out a lot that's surprised me, Gavin."

Gavin steeled his spine for what was to come. "Like?"

"Like you're not registered with Doctors Without Borders."

"No."

"Yet Becca has said for months that you were out of the country most of the time, which was why you weren't available to meet us. And the reason for the elopement. She said you were about to go into a country that was dangerous."

"She was stalling, I believe." They walked between two tall buildings, blocking the sunlight. The temperature dropped immediately.

"Why would she do that?"

Gavin looked directly at him, taking in how ill he looked, but Gavin was sure Eric wouldn't want the discussion interrupted with questions about his health.

"She felt pressured by you and your brothers,"

Gavin said. "She's felt pressured for years, apparently. You all tried to set her up on blind dates, even when she asked you not to. You haven't treated her as an adult, but your kid sister. I get that—I have a couple of younger sisters myself—but she reached the end of her rope with your interference. I think she wanted us to have time to ourselves to see where our relationship was going first, so she made up a story so that you and I wouldn't meet."

Confusion registered in Eric's eyes. "I'm stunned, Gavin. Really. We've only been protecting her. Our parents weren't around to do that."

"Protecting shouldn't mean smothering, and that's how she's felt. She's thirty years old. She's got an MBA from Wharton. She's a cofounder of a successful, cutting-edge business. She negotiates deals, Eric. Big ones. She supports herself just fine. You all need to take a second look at who she's become and back off."

"Back off? We've been trying to save her."

"How? From what? I don't get it."

Eric shoved his hands through his hair. "She never slows down. Never. She's always in such a hurry—no, a *frenzy* to get things done. We figured the right man could get her to slow down. We thought she was on her way to a big crash. We were doing everything we could to prevent that. If that's interference, so be it."

"I could see that, too," Gavin said quietly. He'd thought all along there was something bizarre about all of them setting her up with dates. She'd misinterpreted. They weren't waiting on her to get settled so that they finally could. They were afraid for her.

Eric surveyed their surroundings, saying nothing. They made another right turn, which meant they were halfway through their walk, therefore halfway through their conversation.

"What about the medical malpractice suit against you?" Eric asked, leaving the subject of Becca's mental health behind.

"It's resolved. I wasn't found liable." *I did what I had to do to save two lives. And now everyone has to live with the consequences.*

"Why are you living with Becca here? You have a home in San Francisco."

"After the hearings ended a couple of weeks ago, I decided to take some time off. It was a grueling experience, plus I've always put in long hours. I needed to recharge."

"When you're done recharging? What then? You'll live there, and she'll live here?"

"That's one option." Gavin was grateful Eric hadn't pushed about the lawsuit. If he opened up to anyone about it, he wanted it to be Becca. In fact, no matter how things worked out today, he would do that, tell her the truth. He owed her that.

"Ah. The weekend marriage. How modern of you." Eric didn't hide his sarcasm. "Hard to make babies that way. But then, you would know all about that, wouldn't you?"

"Everything you've said and asked has sounded like an accusation. Why?"

"Because this is my sister we're talking about. There's no one in the world I love more. I don't want her hurt."

And your sister doesn't want children. "No one can promise that."

"I know." His voice was raspy, full of emotion.

They made another turn.

Almost there, Gavin thought. The conversation had to come to an end soon.

"Something else bothers me," Eric said.

Gavin waited.

"I understand you own a nice house in San Francisco, but...roommates, Gavin? Really? At your age and with your professional status?"

Gavin was tired of the intrusion into his life. He wasn't married to the man's sister. He was a temporary husband for hire, bought and paid for. At least this time he could tell the truth.

"That house was the best investment I've made. I bought it with the intention of using it as income property while I was doing my residency, and, yes, I've had roommates all along, fellow residents, now full-time practicing physicians. I worked pretty much all the time. So did they. We rarely saw each other. But two of them have moved on, and the last one is getting married next month, so the house will be all mine. I don't have a moment's regret for doing that."

After Gavin wrapped up his speech he clamped his mouth shut. He was done with this conversation. He couldn't stand up to Eric without harming Becca's relationship with him.

"My apologies," Eric said. "I jumped to conclusions. It's a bad habit of mine."

Gavin shifted his shoulders, but said nothing.

"Look," Eric said, his voice softening. "I've kept a close eye on you, both of you, since I got here yesterday. I like what I see. You've been good for her, there's no doubt about that. Her house is in order, but more important, she's happy. It's obvious how much she loves you, and you her."

It stopped Gavin cold, hearing that. If Eric thought Becca had fallen in love, they'd pulled it off. They'd given a masterful performance.

Why, then, did it feel so wrong? And deceitful? *Low.*

They made the final turn onto her street, came to her lobby door. Eric stopped there and put out his hand.

"Thank you for what you've done for her. And welcome to the family."

Now Gavin felt lower than low as he returned Eric's handshake. "Thank you," he said simply.

"One last thing," Eric said. "I'll be giving her your wedding gift as soon as we go back upstairs. I'm counting on you to make sure it gets used."

With that enigmatic statement, they went inside and upstairs. When they entered the loft, Becca turned in her chair. Her smile looked a little sick. He didn't rush across the room. There wasn't much he could say or do that wouldn't be seen by the three men still seated at the dining table with her. Couldn't give her a thumbs-up. Couldn't wipe his brow as if relieved. In fact, he didn't know if Eric would say something that would come as a shock to Becca, either, and how she would handle it.

"I challenged him to a duel," Eric said behind him, saving the day. "It was a tie." Then, there was a moment of silence before he spoke again. "I couldn't have chosen a better husband for you if I'd picked him myself, Bec."

Her smile lit up the room. "Thank you." She hurried to him, giving him a hug. "I'm glad."

"It'll make life easier, I know," Eric said drily, then he angled back and looked at her. "Now it's your turn."

Eric didn't take her outdoors but to her bedroom. She sat on the bed as he wandered around the room, examining the photographs on her dresser, peeking into her closet, which she hadn't shut. Gavin's clothes were visible.

"It's good to see your loft is finally a home," he said, taking a seat on the chaise, still looking pale and wobbly.

"I know. I can't believe I let it sit like that for five months. Gavin took care of everything," she said, giving credit where credit was due.

"He also says you're still debating about your living arrangements in the future."

"That's right." She wished she knew exactly what they talked about so that she could match Gavin's stories. All she could do was trust that their separate stories held up.

"It must be hard, with your job being here and his practice being in San Francisco."

So far, so good, she thought. "We'll figure it out."

"Well, if you end up wanting to sell this place, let me know. I might be interested."

That caught her off guard. "So, you were serious about moving here?"

"I need to get out of New York. And now that you're settled, I can start looking for the same thing you have. I've found myself missing my family." He shifted in his seat. "Or would you rather I didn't move here?"

He looked sad. Maybe heartbroken? He'd always loved the hustle and bustle of New York, so to leave it was huge. What happened to change his mind?

"I would love to have you close by, Eric. All four of you. No question." Which was the truth. She just didn't see how she could maintain her pretend marriage for any length of time. The lie seemed worth it now that Eric appeared to be moving forward with his life. She'd met her goal.

"Gavin tells me we've smothered you," Eric said. "Me, especially."

She didn't know what to say to that. She didn't know in what context Gavin had made that point.

"I missed walking you down the aisle, and that hurts, Bec. I wish you'd been honest with me. I wish you hadn't felt like you needed to elope."

The last thing she wanted was for them to end the visit with an argument, but she also needed to take advantage of the opening to make her point. She wouldn't be "married" for long. "How many times did I ask you to back off, Eric? Lots and lots. You never took me seriously."

He nodded, then he turned his head and swallowed. "I'm sorry I screwed up with you. Does it help to know that my heart was in the right place?"

She rushed over to him and hugged him hard. "Yes. But I never doubted that. I owe you a lot, Eric. A whole lot. But not control of my life."

He squeezed her tight, then let her go. She sat beside him, bumping shoulders. "I love you."

He kissed her head. "I love you, too. It's hard to give up worrying about you. But I like your Gavin. He'll do you well." He pulled an envelope from his back pocket and handed it to her.

"What's this?"

"There are two items in there. The letter explains everything. We want you to take a honeymoon, so we arranged a place for you to go. I gather that Gavin is free at the moment."

Guilt stomped on her. Last weekend she'd had the wedding without the honeymoon, at least for the photographs. Now the honeymoon without the wedding? How was she going to get out of this? Because there was absolutely no way she was going anywhere. She had work to do and— Well, they just wouldn't go. Gavin would support her in that. She didn't want to argue with Eric right now.

"The second is a check that represents your trust fund from Mom and Dad."

She opened the envelope and looked inside…and almost choked on the amount written on the check. "Did you…did everyone get a check like this?"

"On their thirtieth birthdays. Yours is the largest because it's been invested untouched the longest, but we've all done well. I should've given it to you on your birthday, but I wanted to do it in person."

"Plus you thought I was being flaky. You didn't think I really had a boyfriend."

"Then you got married without us," he said softly, but with obvious pain. "I wanted to make sure your boyfriend and then husband wasn't a gold digger. You need to talk to a lawyer who specializes in this sort of thing. This money is personally yours."

Becca wondered how Eric was going to feel when—if—he learned the truth. He would've proven himself right, that she *was* flaky.

She was tempted to blurt out the truth. All of it. But they'd had a good weekend, and he was finally acknowledging her as an adult. He seemed happy— except for how he'd said he needed to get out of New York City. Why?

He patted her knee. "We should head to the airport."

"This has been such a great weekend," she said. "Even though you got sick. At least you won't have to stay at a hotel after this, now that the guest room is finally available."

They rejoined the men. Sam was tipped back in his chair, smiling, as Trent laughed. Buckled over, Jeff slapped his thigh.

Gavin grinned. He looked happy and comfortable as she came up beside him and set her hand on his shoulder. He put his arm around her, his hand resting on her hip, his brows raised slightly as if in question. She winked. He squeezed her hip then, and the conversation started up again, apparently another story of Becca as a child, this time how she and Jeff had played barber as kids, and who knew that children's plastic scissors could cut so well?

Trent had scanned the family photo of the event into his cell phone so that he could show her new husband how she'd looked with her previously long hair cut into choppy lengths. She remembered her mother screaming when she saw her.

Becca didn't mind being the subject of laughter. In fact, she would think something was wrong if they didn't tease her mercilessly. That was her role as the little sister.

She looked at each of them, her heart swelling. She loved them all so much. She hoped they would stop worrying about her now and move forward with their lives. Eric had just admitted to her that he'd put his life on hold somewhat, wanting to be sure she was taken care of. Now he could.

Although if he moved to Sacramento very soon—

"Time to go," Eric said. "We have planes to catch, and the lovebirds need to pack and get going."

Becca waited for Gavin to intervene. When he didn't, she said, "Although I really appreciate your gift, this isn't a good time for me. I've got two big deals coming up and two new clients on board. Maybe later."

"I already cleared it with Chip," Eric said.

Becca only saw red. "You what?" She turned to Gavin. "See? See what I have to put up with? Now he's interfering in my business life on top of my personal life. *And* he's got Chip interfering, too."

She rounded on Eric. All the men had gone silent. "I'm not going anywhere. I fly all the time. I'm sick of it. Traveling is not fun anymore."

"Which is why we rented a cabin in the mountains for you. It's only an hour's drive, Bec. No airports. No hassle. Don't you both deserve a honeymoon?"

"We do," Gavin said, putting his arm around her waist. "Thank you."

Thus the visit ended on a tense note instead of a happy one. A few minutes later, the loft was quiet again, and Gavin and Becca were facing the aftermath of their lie—and the question mark of their future.

"We're not going anywhere," she said, her arms crossed.

"I don't see how we can get out of it. You know Eric will check to make sure we're there."

She couldn't decide how Gavin felt about it. "You want to go?"

"Frankly I could use a change of scenery. And I can't think of anyone better to share it with." He moved in on her, cupped her shoulders. "We started something last night. Let's end it the right way. We have to live this lie a little longer to make it believable, anyway, so let's do this. We can repay them later."

She couldn't. She really couldn't. She would fall all the way in love with him, and maybe he would fall in love with her. They didn't want the same things. One of them, maybe both of them, would get hurt.

"I can't," she said, going up on tiptoe and kissing him softly.

Her doorbell rang. She looked through the peephole and groaned. "It's Eric," she whispered. "He's probably going to stay here until we leave. We should start calling him The Enforcer."

He banged on the door. "Becca!"

Gavin reached around her and opened the door. Eric raced through, going straight to the bathroom. When he finally emerged, he leaned against the doorjamb. "I can't fly. Since you're not going to be around, do you mind if I stay here until I can?"

"We don't mind at all," Gavin said as Becca pinched his waist.

"Bec?"

She'd been cornered. Whether on purpose or accident, she had no choice now. "Of course you're welcome to stay, Eric."

Chapter Twelve

Gavin carried Eric's suitcase into the guest room. "I'm not completely comfortable leaving you here alone," Gavin said. "If it's food poisoning, which I suspect it is, you just need to rest and stay hydrated. If it's more than that…"

"I won't hesitate to get myself to a doctor. Scout's honor."

"Call us now and then, please. Let us know how you're doing."

"I will. Thanks for getting Bec to go on the trip."

My pleasure, Gavin thought. "You're right. She needs some downtime. It's not surprising she had to be forced to take it."

"I'm probably not high on her list at the moment."

Gavin smiled but didn't confirm Eric's statement. "She'll get over it. I've got to run a few errands before we can leave. Can I get you anything?"

"Ginger ale? I know it probably doesn't do anything, but it's what my mother always gave us when we were sick."

"Ginger has stomach-soothing properties. And comfort foods help in ways we don't even understand. I'll pop in on you before we head out."

He shut the door, then spotted Becca sitting at the dining-room table, her chin propped on her fists. "How's he doing?" she asked.

"Sounds like he needs a day or two before he should travel."

"I feel like I should be here. You know. To take care of him."

Gavin laughed. "Nice try. You're going on the trip."

She didn't stick out her tongue, but she might as well have.

He laid a hand on her shoulder. "I need to go pick up the rest of my things and run a couple of errands," he said. Actually he hoped to catch a little sleep. He was dog tired. "I'll come back when I'm done and we can head out."

"Okay. I need to spend some time on the phone with Suki, anyway. Tell her what's in the works for the week."

She sounded glum, but actually better than earlier. "Think of it as an adventure." He leaned over and kissed her, careful to keep it from escalating. Not now. Not yet. Tonight. They would have all the freedom and privacy they wanted, and in a place that didn't have personal meaning to either of them. "I'll be back in two hours. I'll also have my cell phone on, if you need me earlier than that."

Gavin ended up too tired to sleep. He tried. For over an hour he tried before giving up. He checked out of the hotel, stopped at a nearby department store to pick up an extra pair of jeans, a sweatshirt and hiking boots, then picked up the ginger ale. Like Becca, he hadn't taken a real vacation in years. He occasionally drove to his hometown to see his family, which he didn't consider vacation, but duty calls—except that he liked his sister Dixie and was always glad to see her. She also occasionally came to the city to see him.

As for Shana, she'd disappeared for ten years, so she hadn't been part of the equation until recently. He was enjoying getting to know her as the woman she'd become. But his parents? The fewer hours he spent with them, the better. His mom was okay, but her world was narrow. His dad's was even more.

So, a vacation was a welcome luxury, and taking it with Becca? Pure indulgence.

He left his suitcase outside the loft door, in case Eric was awake.

"How's your brother?" he asked Becca when he got inside.

"Still sleeping."

Gavin grabbed the suitcase from the hall and quickly carried it into the bedroom, then put the ginger ale in the refrigerator. "I need to add the things I left here to my bag. Are you packed?"

"All set," she said. She finally looked as if she wanted to go. He, however, felt like wagging his tail.

"We'll need to pick up groceries," she said. "We'll be at a cabin in the woods. No restaurant. No room service. The brochure Eric added lists nearby places of interest, and there's a market, but apparently it's small."

"Well, then, why don't we shop here in town, put everything in ice chests and take them along. We won't have to go anywhere for a while, at least. We'll have to use your car, since mine won't hold everything."

"That's fine. I have a full tank."

He took her face in his hands and kissed her, this time letting it go deeper, arousing her. Arousing himself. "Thanks for doing this," he said against her lips before she could say, "Like I had a choice."

He wanted to believe that, ultimately, she did have a choice—just an almost impossible one.

She nodded, her eyes closed, her lips still parted. Damn if she wasn't the sexiest woman...

"I'm looking forward to tonight," he said, lifting his head.

"And here I thought you were so adventurous," she said, mischief in her voice. She leaned into him. "I'm looking forward to this *afternoon*," she whispered dramatically.

"Eager, are you?"

"Too eager to wait for nightfall. Unless you have some objection." She walked away, her hips moving sassily.

He appreciated her confidence. "No, your honor. No objection from me."

"Good. Because I would've had to overrule it. Now, you go pack your bag. Let's get this honey—I mean, vacation on the road."

They both went quiet. They were deceiving themselves to think this was anything other than a weeklong trip together to unwind after the weeklong ruse. They would enjoy their mutual attraction and not have lingering, unmet needs. They were adults, capable of embarking on this journey, then ending it civilly.

"Yes," he said. "Let's get going."

Two hours later, unease settled over Gavin, poking dread into him with sharp pinpricks. It had taken them an hour to shop, and she'd said it would take an hour to get to their location, which meant they were close now.

The problem was, he knew this area well. These foothills were where he grew up, in a small town called Chance City, only two exits away.

Had Eric known that?

No. Why would he send them where people would know them? What kind of honeymoon would that be?

Gavin should've asked where they were going. But because they hadn't chosen it themselves and the plans were already set, he'd figured it didn't matter.

Becca was consulting the directions she'd been given but didn't tell him to turn off. They passed the first exit. Then the second. Gavin relaxed. There were lots of beautiful, rustic Mother Lode towns in the area just as picturesque as Chance City, and where they wouldn't run into an entire population he'd known since birth.

"Take the next exit," Becca said.

Not far enough. Not nearly far enough, Gavin thought. He couldn't even form any words, just listened and followed her directions to the rental, although Gavin was pretty sure he knew where they would end up. Becca would be thrilled with Eric's choice. It was the perfect place, meeting all their needs. A secluded cabin in the woods, but with all the comforts of home.

And it was owned by a friend of his, Jake McCoy, whose younger brother Joe was married to Gavin's sister Dixie.

"Oh! Isn't this beautiful," Becca said as a perfect little cabin came into view. She opened the car door, stepped out and admired the view. A cool breeze lifted her hair, filling her head with the earthy fragrances of the land. They were surrounded by tall pines and old, enormous oaks bearing new spring growth. Small boulders nestled amongst manzanitas. Two Adirondack chairs sat side by side on the porch that wrapped around the whole building, the rustic railing ideal for the log cabin that suited the landscape perfectly.

Becca rushed up the stairs and plopped into one of the chairs. "They're not rockers, but they're perfect. Look at the view."

It just occurred to her that Gavin had gone quiet. Didn't he like the place? It seemed just right to her.

She got out of the chair and met him at the car where he was unloading the trunk. "Are you okay?" she asked. "Maybe the cabin is too secluded for you?" He was a city boy, after all.

"It's fine," he said, then he set an ice chest on the ground, took her by the shoulders and kissed her. "No, it's not just fine. It's spectacular. Eric did a great job."

She smiled, relieved. He was probably tired. Neither of them had slept much last night. "It looks like we can start a hike to all different directions from here, doesn't it? And everything is so green. I'll open up then come back to help carry."

She grabbed one suitcase to take with her, located the key under the welcome mat and opened the door wide. The place smelled of lemon oil and wood, and it was dark enough, even during midafternoon, to need lights turned on. A man's space, she thought, taking in the huge rock fireplace, contemporary kitchen and big-screen television. The furnishings were cabin decor and masculine, mostly leather and wood, a look she appreciated. She figured it would be cold enough at night to light a fire. There was plenty of wood stacked under the porch.

Becca heard Gavin's footsteps as he climbed the stairs then came into the living room. His expression serious, he went straight to the kitchen with the largest ice chest, then he grinned at her as he headed to the door again. Okay, she thought. Everything was okay. She'd been imagining…something.

They brought everything inside and put it all away, making quick work of it. There were two bedrooms, the master containing a king-size bed. The bathroom wasn't luxurious but had a large shower and tub combination. Everything was spotless.

"Are you hungry?" she asked.

"Starved."

His tone and expression indicated he wasn't talking about food. Becca was fine with that. She'd come to this trip without illusions. She knew she was probably going to have her heart broken, but she could deal with that. She would just immerse herself in work again and focus. Any pain she felt would resolve itself in time.

She hadn't planned on falling in love with someone so right and yet so wrong for her. The most important thing was making sure he didn't get hurt, especially since he already seemed to be hurting about something.

Although she was pretty sure he had a lot of doubts, too, about her, given how they'd started this relationship to perpetuate a lie she'd created.

They could work it out during the week, she hoped. For now it was all about the freedom they'd been given to enjoy each other. It was just them, alone, without the pressure of work or getting her house in order or sustaining a lie or playing a part. She intended to take full advantage of the situation.

"If you have to take an hour to make up your mind, Becca…"

She jolted. Then before she could pull his shirt off, he scooped her into his arms and carried her into the bedroom. The bedding was folded down—when had he done that? He put a knee on the bed, lowering her to the mattress, following her down, stretching out beside her. He hadn't kissed her yet. She was dying to be kissed.

He removed her clothes but stayed dressed himself, which seemed unfair…and totally erotic.

"You have amazing skin," he said, running his hands down her from neck to toe, leisurely, deliberately, his intention obviously to arouse, not satisfy. He explored, stimulated, awakened, electrifying every nerve ending. When he was done using his hands, his mouth took over, lips and tongue, hot and wet, searching, seeking, discovering. Still not kissing her…

He cherished her breasts, lavished her nipples at the same time his fingers were busy sliding down her abdomen and beyond, then pulling back when she got close to climax, only to return to the torture again. And still no kiss.

When she thought she couldn't survive another moment, he rolled her over and treated her backside to the same unhurried treatment, his fingers delving, tormenting.

She made a quick roll onto her back, looked into his aroused and amused gaze. "You need to get naked."

"But I'm enjoying this. Aren't you?"

"You're not expecting an answer, are you?" Getting to her knees, she lifted his polo shirt over his head and tossed it aside. She watched his face as she unzipped his jeans.

"That's better," he said, closing his eyes a moment.

"No one was forcing you to suffer," she said with a smile, delighted with everything. All of it. All of him...

She wanted to enjoy him, to take as much time as he had, but that was going to have to wait for another time, sometime when she could find some patience.

Not now.

She helped him finish undressing then she lay back, extending her arms in welcome and demand. He covered her body with his.

"I thought you were beautiful last night," he said, nibbling at her lips. "But daylight shows how truly magnificent you are."

She couldn't remember being told she was beautiful, much less magnificent. The praise overwhelmed her. She threaded his soft, shiny hair with her fingers then splayed them against his head. "Come inside me," she whispered.

"I aim only to please," he said, kissing her finally, sliding into her, filling her.

"A perfect fit," she murmured, arching and sinking in rhythm, oblivious to everything except him.

"Yes," he murmured back.

"Made for each other."

She'd gone too far, said too much. She knew it the moment the words were out of her mouth. He jerked a little, seemed ready to pull away. She tightened her arms, squeezed him from inside and out. He got back into the rhythm, soared high with her as sweat adhered them to each other, groaned as long and loud as she did. As good as last night was, it was nothing compared to this, this drawn-out, potent, intoxicating moment.

She would remember this for the rest of her life.

He finally draped his body over hers for a few seconds then rolled onto his side, taking her with him. With his feet he grabbed the bedding and inched it up. She reached down, pulled it over their shoulders. Then they relaxed into each other, sated.

She didn't know what to say. Should she apologize

for her outburst? Even though it was true, it wasn't what their relationship was about.

Her fretting didn't lead to any answers, then she realized he'd fallen asleep.

She closed her eyes and joined him, naked, entwined and feeling happier than she had in a very long time.

Gavin tried to grab hold of something, anything, but there was only open sky. No lifeline. No safety net. He struggled, he fought, he strained. His world spun as he plummeted. Was he falling faster or was the bottom rising? Or both?

"Gavin!"

A hitch in his fall, like the wind had come up, shifting him sideways…

"Gavin, wake up. You're dreaming. Wake up!"

Becca. Her voice was coated with fear. Of him?

Flat on his back, he opened his eyes, lying still, registering his surroundings. The bedding was in tangles, jumbled around his feet.

"Are you okay?" Becca asked. Naked, she was kneeling next to him. He was also naked…and vulnerable.

"Yes." He grabbed her hand, pressed it against his chest, held it there, needing the connection.

"Your heart's thundering. You were having a nightmare. It seemed…horrible."

"It was." He pulled her down next to him, tucked her close. Even accustomed to the nightmares, he knew this one had been particularly bad. If she hadn't woken him up, would he have hit ground?

"Do you have nightmares a lot?" she asked, her hand still resting right over his heart, but not moving, just being there, offering more comfort than she could ever imagine.

"Yes." She might as well know that much, since she was bound to see him have more. The wide-awake ones he had were bad, too. If she'd noticed those, she hadn't said anything.

She didn't say anything now, either, but her expression said everything.

"I'm okay." He brushed his lips against her hair. "Were you scared?"

"Not for myself. You weren't violent. But, yes, I was scared for you. You seemed so…lost."

Lost. It was a good word. He'd been lost and wandering for quite a while, even before the lawsuit, actually. He'd come to realize that after watching how hard Becca worked, how many hours she put in. He'd been like that, maybe worse.

He needed to get her to see how much damage it could cause, then get her to make changes. That would be his final task and the most important thing he could do for her. Yes, he'd played the part of her husband. And yes, he'd helped organize her life. But none of that mattered compared to getting her to slow down, to not become like him.

Her brothers needed that to happen, too. And Chip, apparently, wanted Becca to change, as well.

She shouldn't have to live with the aftermath of pushing too hard.

So, he would keep his secret to himself a little longer. He would get her to play, to rediscover fun. That accomplishment would be his reward.

"What time is it?" he asked, looking for a clock, not finding one.

She rolled away from him, grabbed her jeans from the floor and pulled out her cell phone. "Six-thirty. We slept for two hours."

He stretched. "I could eat a horse. Or, in this case, that rotisserie chicken we bought." He got out of bed, pulled on his jeans and shirt, enjoying the sight of her getting dressed, too.

The furrow between her brows hadn't gone away completely yet. It was nice to have someone worry about him, but he didn't want her babying him.

"You're in charge of salad," he said.

"We bought premade potato salad."

"You can manage that, right?" He laughed when she tossed a pillow at him, caught it easily and fired it back, scooping up the second pillow, making it a real pillow fight that lasted until they both collapsed. Then hand in hand, they left the bedroom.

"Were you a Boy Scout?" she asked.

"Why?"

"I'm hoping you know how to lay a fire. I really want to cozy in with a fire."

"Of course, ma'am." He pretended to tip a hat. "I'd be more'n happy to."

She laughed. They carried on a cowboy and the lady routine while they dished up dinner then took their plates outside to watch the sunset, having to wear their sweatshirts as the temperature had dropped quickly.

He built a fire while she did the dishes. Then they settled on the couch to watch the flames.

"I don't mind if you want to turn on the TV," she said. "Are you a Giants fan? There's probably a game on."

"I'm good, thanks. Do you feel like you're unwinding?"

"Definitely."

"How many times have you thought about work?"

"Do I have to tell the truth?" She tucked her feet up beside her and laid her head on his shoulder.

"That many times, huh?"

"It's probably more than you would like, but less than you think."

"Well, that made a lot of sense."

"It did to me."

He smiled into her hair. "Would you like to go for a hike in the morning?"

"Absolutely. This is beautiful country. I hope you have a good sense of direction because mine stinks."

"I think I can manage not to get us lost." He'd roamed these woods since he was a kid.

One by one she got text messages from her

brothers, saying they were home. Eric texted, too, that he was hanging in there. She told each of them thanks for the honeymoon, that they were already enjoying themselves.

No one texted Gavin. His sister Dixie was halfway around the world, time zones away. Shana had Emma to take care of, to fill her hours. His parents didn't own a cell phone. Even if they had, texting would be beyond their abilities. They never called, anyway. He always had to call them.

His partners were leaving him alone, as he'd requested. Other friends from San Francisco had left messages he hadn't answered in weeks. They'd probably given up on him. He didn't blame them.

But even with the nightmare this afternoon, Gavin could see a light at the end of his long, dark tunnel. He felt...hopeful.

He never would've imagined that participating in a big lie would end up bringing him the peace he'd been craving.

Chapter Thirteen

"You said you wouldn't get us lost!" Becca searched the surroundings with her eyes, panicked. They'd been hiking for a couple of hours, had scared off birds, deer and other low-to-the-ground creatures that were gone before she could identify them. Squirrels hopped branch to branch everywhere they went, startling her.

Gavin looked up. "I know the direction we need to go, based on where the sun is. This way. I think."

"City boy," she muttered.

"Isn't that a case of the pot calling the kettle black?"

"I never said I was anything *other* than a city girl.

I wasn't the one feeling confident about hiking in the woods."

He hugged her. "There, there."

"Don't you dare be condescending."

"I wouldn't dream of it." He passed her a granola bar then surveyed the land. "For the record, I've only been a city boy since I turned eighteen. I grew up in country very much like this."

"I never would've guessed. Of course you've barely said a word about your past, just hints. I, on the other hand, have been an open book."

He shrugged. "Different styles."

"No, Gavin, it's a choice people make, what to share and what to hold back."

"We haven't known each other long enough to have shared a whole lot."

"Not even the basics? Like where you grew up? What's the harm in that?" She was becoming increasingly anxious. She'd surreptitiously checked her cell phone a while back, finding no bars. They couldn't even call for help. "I don't see how— What was that?"

He looked in the same direction. A large creature zipped by not far from them.

"Was that a wolf?" she asked, inching closer to him.

"There aren't any wolves here. Coyote, maybe."

"Coyote?" She looked hard, listened harder, not seeing or hearing the beast again.

"They're around these parts, but they're also nocturnal. Should be sleeping at this time of day, though. Unless it's sick…"

She grabbed his arm and shook him, then clung to him. "Why didn't we leave breadcrumbs?"

"Because the coyote would've eaten them." He grinned. "It was probably a dog, Becca. We're very close to civilization, actually."

They heard an animal yelp and then whimper. Gavin took off toward the sound. Becca, not wanting to be left alone, followed. They found a medium-size, furry brown dog of the mutt variety, with a cute face, its tail tucked between its legs. It held its right front paw off the ground. Seeing the dog up close now, she realized it was much smaller than her active imagination had conjured it to be.

Gavin eased toward it. The animal tried to back up, but yelped again when it set its paw down. "It's okay," Gavin said gently. "I won't hurt you."

"It could have rabies," she whispered loudly.

"It's wearing a collar." He crouched, then got closer, made more soothing sounds. "Probably picked up a burr in its paw."

The dog sniffed the air.

"It's wary of you," Gavin said calmly. "Try to relax."

She could try to, but she wasn't getting low to the ground like Gavin and risk getting bitten in the face, dog collar or not.

The dog kept its eyes more on her than Gavin, who finally got close enough to touch. He gently petted the dog, speaking quietly, soothingly. The dog finally lay down, almost dropped to the ground, actually, as if it couldn't stay upright a second longer.

Gavin ran his hands over him, lightly, competently. He yelped when its right front paw was touched. "It's okay, boy," he said, having determined his gender. "Let me look."

The dog whimpered but allowed Gavin's examination, his eyes full of pain, making Becca tear up.

"He's got several burrs embedded. Must've stepped in a clump of clover," Gavin said.

"Can you get them out?"

"Not here. We should take him back to the cabin and deal with it there."

"Deal with it, as in get in the car and find a vet?"

"That's an option." He gently scooped the dog into his arms. "Let's go."

"You know where you're going?"

"Of course I know where I'm going."

She stopped and plunked her fists on her hips. "You let me think we were lost."

"*You* thought that. I said I knew where to head." He looked over the dog's head at her, his eyes sparkling. "We're only ten minutes away or so, city girl."

Instead of being irritated, she actually loved the way he was looking at her, obviously having fun with her. He probably hadn't appreciated having his abilities challenged, so he'd played her a little.

"I guess you didn't like being called a city boy,"

she said, eyeing the dog, wondering if he would let her pet him, deciding not to test it.

"I wouldn't have taken you hiking if I didn't know I could get you safely home."

She had nothing to say to that. He'd wanted her to trust him, and she had—to a point. But really, it'd been her own fears about getting lost that had driven her to believe otherwise, to *disbelieve* him. Beneath his outward humor was an inward disappointment that she hadn't had faith in him.

Had he been challenged by that before? Had someone lost faith in him, someone who mattered?

He was a man of many layers, some she'd come to recognize and appreciate, some he hadn't yet revealed. If she hadn't grown up with brothers, she might not have understood how much men needed to feel respected and trusted.

They reached the cabin. "You know the towel you keep in your trunk? Could you get that, please? And do you have tweezers? And manicure scissors, maybe? If not, maybe there are scissors somewhere in the house."

"So, we're not taking him to the vet?"

"Not yet."

She got the towel, then headed inside to get her tweezers.

"Bring my overnight kit, too, would you?"

She returned with the items. He swaddled the dog before carrying him inside, setting him on the dining-room table. Gavin gave orders as if he'd been born to, calmly, confidently, expecting her to obey, all the while keeping the nervous dog from sprinting off. Becca held him while Gavin worked on his paw, trimming the fur between the dog's toes, then ever so gently pulling out six burrs, one at a time, a necessarily long, slow process so that nothing broke off in his foot, where it could become embedded. When Gavin was satisfied he'd gotten all of them, he doused the footpads with hydrogen peroxide, then checked all the other paws.

"I don't know anyone else who carries hydrogen peroxide with them, and you weren't even a Boy Scout," she said, pleased when he laughed. "You did a great job, Gavin. I guess working in a hospital paid off. And you," she said to the dog. "You are one lucky pooch."

His tail thumped the table.

Gavin lifted him down to the floor. He lowered his paw gingerly, tested it, then finally left it down. He wagged his tail, gave Gavin a big lick on the face then pranced around the room, his paw seeming a little tender still, but obviously much better.

"He's got a collar but no tags," Becca said, smiling at how happy the dog was. "He looks hungry. Should I feed him some of our chicken?"

"I imagine you'll get a lick on the face for that."

She'd barely gotten it out of the refrigerator when the dog came running. "Nothing wrong with his sniffer," she said, laughing as he nudged her leg with his muzzle. He ate as fast as she could pull meat off the carcass. "What are we going to do with him?"

Gavin leaned against the kitchen counter and watched her fill a bowl of water and put it on the floor. The dog lapped it noisily until it was all gone then he finally sat, his tongue lolling to one side. He looked ready to sleep sitting up.

"Maybe you could fix him a bed of some sorts? Or put the towel in front of the hearth? I think he'll sleep. I'll make some phone calls and see if I can locate the owner."

"How do you do that?"

"The lost-and-found posts in the newspaper. The animal shelter." Although Gavin knew exactly who to call. The Take a Lode Off Diner was the lifeblood of Chance City. If someone in town was missing a dog, the diner's owner, Honey, would know about it.

He located the phone book and found the number while Becca made a bed for the dog, who looked at her then at the towel then back at her again, as if saying, "Who, me? Lie on that? I need something soft, lady! I'm an invalid."

Becca tried lying down on the towel herself and patting the floor. The dog simply watched her, then after a moment jumped on the couch and plopped, almost asleep before his head hit the cushions.

"Good thing the couch is leather," she said, kneeling down and petting the dog then pulling back, waving a hand in front of her face. "Phew. He needs a bath."

She went off toward the bathroom to wash her hands.

Gavin found the number for the diner. He didn't think Honey would recognize his voice. He hadn't been there often in the years since he'd left home. But just in case he walked outside with his phone.

"Take a Lode Off," Honey answered in her distinctive voice.

"Hi. I'm vacationing just outside of your town, and I found a dog wandering around who looked lost. He has a collar but no tags."

She didn't even question why he was calling her diner. "It wouldn't be a brown dog with long fur and a friendly smile, would it? Red collar?"

"That's him." What a relief. Except, what a problem, too. How was he going to return a dog if he knew the owner? "Can you give me the number of the owner?"

"Dial 1-800-HEAVEN, I guess. She died about a month ago. Her next-door neighbor said he'd take Pancho—that's the dog's name—but Pancho won't have anything to do with him. He runs off, comes back to be fed now and then, then he disappears again for days.... Hold your horses, Jake McCoy! Can't you see I'm on the phone," she yelled, loud enough for Gavin to hold his phone away from his ear. "Sorry 'bout that. It's lunchtime at the OK Corral. If you want to bring the dog here, I'll make sure he gets to the right person, although I'm guessing he'll end up at the shelter this time. Who knows? Maybe someone will adopt the incorrigible thing."

Gavin covered the phone as he laughed. He knew Honey well enough to get that she was playing on his sympathies. She wouldn't take the dog to the shelter. She probably figured, as Gavin did now, that the dog was mourning his mistress.

"I'll give you a call later," he said. "If that's okay. Give you time to ask around."

"Suit yourself. Bye now."

Gavin returned to the cabin. Becca was curled in a chair, dozing. The dog's snore sounded loud in the quiet room.

"His name is Pancho," Gavin said to Becca as she roused herself and stretched.

"You found his owner? That's great!"

"Unfortunately the owner passed away. Dog's been playing hide-and-seek ever since. The person I talked to said Pancho would have to go to the shelter."

Becca's face fell. "No. That can't happen. We have to find a home for him."

"We? You live in a loft and are gone ten to twelve hours a day. My life is similar."

"I know. But we can ask around. He's a sweet dog." Her voice got quiet. "I've never had a dog, or a pet of any kind. Jeff is allergic to animal fur. He always felt so bad for the rest of us, and we pretended it didn't matter."

Aha. Hence, the dog-figurine collection, Gavin decided, her way of coping with the loss of something she wanted badly. Which didn't account for why she wouldn't take them out of the box, however.

"I never owned a pet, either. Shana begged for a kitten every Christmas, but Dad said no."

"Does she have one now?"

"Not that I'm aware of." He scratched his head. "Well, it looks like we'd better pick up some dog supplies. Do you want to go or stay here with Pancho?"

"I'll stay. I don't want him to get worried when he wakes up alone."

Gavin rested his hands on the arms of her chair and leaned over her. "You'd make a good mother." He kissed her before she could say anything, a slow, soft, lingering kiss.

"No, I wouldn't. I don't have a lot of maternal skills," she said, her hands against his face, holding him there, kissing him back.

"You have the most important qualities, and you'd learn the rest." He straightened. "Now, what do you think? Dog food, bowls, a leash?"

"Doggy shampoo."

"Definitely. And a brush." He took the keys she offered. "I won't be too long."

"Toys," she called out as he left.

He didn't drive into Chance City but to Grass Valley, a few miles the other direction. With a population closer to eleven thousand as opposed to Chance City's under two thousand, the odds were better of not being recognized.

At least they didn't know where he was staying.

His cell phone rang just after he loaded everything into the car. He looked at the screen. It was the diner. He couldn't not answer. What if someone wanted the dog?

"Hello?"

"Gavin, this is Jake McCoy."

Gavin almost groaned. "Since when did Honey get caller ID?" He could've blocked the ID feature on his phone except he'd never in a million years expected Honey to succumb to technology. She still hadn't bought a digital cash register.

"Since she had a month of prank calls. They finally stopped, so she's stopped looking at the screen first. Saw your name when she was hanging up. She said you called yourself a visitor. Were you trying to hide your identity?"

"Sort of."

"I'm going to take a big leap here and say that you must be renting my cabin?"

"Right."

"Why didn't you just call me directly? I would've given you a family discount."

Gavin smiled. "If you gave discounts to every family member and extended family member, you'd never make any money. Anyway, a friend made the reservations. I didn't know we were coming here until we pulled into the driveway."

"Yeah? What a coincidence. And now you've got Pancho?"

"Tell me you want him. You've got a little girl who'd love him, I'm sure."

"I don't think that dog'll stay anywhere, with anyone."

"He's in mourning, I figure. Whose dog was he?"

"Grandma Maguire."

"Oh. I'm sorry. I hadn't heard. I liked her. She gave out the best Halloween treats." Everyone had called her Grandma, an honorary title of respect for a woman who'd never married or had children, but who'd always looked out for the townspeople, especially the children. "She must've been about a hundred."

"Ninety-seven. So, hey, do you want to come to dinner one night this week? I'd love for you to get to know Keri. I could ask Donovan and Laura to could come, too. We'll raise our glasses to our brother and your sister."

"Thanks, but not this week. In fact, I'd appreciate it if you don't tell anyone I'm here. We'd like to be alone, you know?"

"Well, I can promise not to tell, but Honey's already spread the word. In the meantime, are you keeping the dog?"

"For now, I guess. But go ahead and ask around. If someone wants him, that'd be great. I don't have room in my life for a dog. It would be really unfair to keep him."

Gavin ended the call and drove back to the cabin,

relieved that Jake had phoned when he did, when the conversation could be kept secret.

Gavin and Becca gave the reluctant Pancho a bath, played ball with him, discovered he took commands well and exhausted themselves. They all fell asleep on the couch in front of the fire.

Sometime around midnight Gavin woke up, roused Becca enough to get her into the bedroom, where he took off her clothes and tucked her into bed, then climbed in after her. She rolled into him, twined her legs and arms with his and went right back to sleep.

Just as Gavin was drifting off, he felt the bed move and knew Pancho had joined them. He didn't have the heart to order the dog to get down.

After a minute Pancho inched closer, set his chin on Gavin's leg and made a little sound of contentment, then so did Becca.

In parenting magazines, it was called the family bed.

He called it crowded. And good.

Chapter Fourteen

Three days later, Gavin sat across the breakfast table from Becca and knew he couldn't—didn't want to—put off telling her the truth any longer. They could deal with it over the last few days of their trip. There was plenty of time to discuss and resolve everything.

He figured she'd get a kick out of having chosen a doctor as her pretend husband, then finding out Gavin was one.

Then again, maybe not. He really didn't have any idea how she would react. He just knew dragging it out any longer wasn't fair to her—or them. He wanted an honest relationship.

He couldn't remember ever being this content, yet

at the same time, wound up. He'd had no responsibilities for days now, and he'd had the freedom to make love whenever they felt like it. Plus no one called or texted. He and Becca didn't go anywhere except for hikes, Pancho trotting alongside them, not even chasing a squirrel, as if he couldn't leave their side.

"How would you like to drive into Chance City today?" he asked Becca.

She looked up from spreading jam on her toast in that precise way she had, edge to edge, then frowned. "We can't leave Pancho here alone."

The dog pricked his ears at the mention of his name. "We'll take him along."

"What if someone recognizes him? Wants to take him?"

"It seems to me Pancho gets to make that decision."

"He *is* a little headstrong, isn't he? And when I checked out the town online, it did look picturesque. Miners settled the place in the 1850s during the gold rush. There must be a lot of great old buildings. When do you want to leave?"

"Whenever you're ready." He'd planned it in his head. They would drive to the middle of town, stop in front of the ice-cream shop. He'd tell her Chance City was where he'd grown up. Across the street was his sister Dixie's salon and spa, Respite. A couple of blocks farther, his parents' hardware store.

He was born here, raised here, grew up to become a doctor. The townspeople were proud of him for that.

He was one of their golden sons, and he'd barely paid attention to them in years.

That would change. He had an obligation to the citizens, one he hadn't been keeping lately.

Now he would. And he would start by telling Becca the truth, being the man his town expected him to be.

"Sit, Pancho. Sit," Becca said as they pulled out of the driveway onto the highway. They'd gone for drives several times during the week, and Pancho had lain down in the backseat, not making any fuss. Today he was up and looking around, worry in his eyes. But this time they were headed south instead of north.

"I think he knows where we're going," she said to Gavin. "He's so smart."

"He is that."

Becca wondered what was going on with Gavin today. He was more restless than she'd ever seen him, *fidgety,* even, a word she never would've applied to him.

Even his eyes were different. Darker, more intense. He flexed his jaw a lot. Everything seemed tied up with the trip to town, because he'd never acted like this before. But why?

"You're quiet," he said, curving his hand over her thigh.

"You, too. I guess we've talked ourselves out. And

I feel like I've finally caught up on my sleep. How about you?"

"I feel rested. And satisfied." He winked at her.

Yes, the lovemaking had been phenomenal. Her body ached pleasantly. Her appetite was bottomless, for food and for him.

"Look at that! Take a Lode Off Diner. Isn't that a cute play on words? What a throwback. I'll bet it's at least seventy years old. We should have lunch there." The central downtown came into view. "Oh, isn't it fantastic? Thank you for bringing me here."

Gavin parked in front of an ice-cream shop. The sidewalks were wood plank, the storefronts shingled, almost like stepping back in time a hundred and fifty years.

They got out of the car, leaving Pancho in it, the windows rolled partway down, but they would also be keeping it in sight. He didn't whimper. Becca figured the last thing he wanted was to be let out here in the place he kept escaping from.

Gavin took her hand and led her to a bench just outside the ice-cream shop.

"What, no ice cream?" she asked.

"I need to talk to you first."

His voice sounded tight, not at all like him.

"What's going on, Gavin?"

"This town, Chance City—"

He stopped talking as a car came hurtling out of control down a side street, heading right toward them. Gavin yanked Becca off the bench and ran, then kept running until the car slammed into the bench, just missing her car with Pancho inside. Gavin let go of her to run back as she stood, shocked, seeing that the car's air bag had deployed and was draped over the steering wheel.

So was a woman.

People poured out of shops and cars and houses. She finally registered the scene enough to pull out her cell phone to dial 911.

"Already called it in," someone said, rushing past her.

"I saw Doc Saxon's car at the Lode," Gavin called out. "Get him."

What? Doc who? Why would Gavin know that?

A teenager raced up the street toward the diner.

The front of the car was completely smashed in, the engine exposed. Becca couldn't tear her gaze away from the surreal scene. Gavin had taken charge and was ordering people around. The driver's door was buckled and jammed. He yanked the passenger door behind it open and climbed in.

"She's pregnant," he called out. "Anyone know her?"

"That's Jennifer Morley," a woman close to Becca yelled. "She's about seven months. I called her husband at work. He's on his way. Here comes Doc Gavin."

Becca spun around, coming face-to-face with Gavin's sister Shana.

"Are you okay?" Shana asked.

She nodded. Nothing made sense. *My parents died in a car crash....*

"Becca?" Shana said. "Do you need to sit down?

She shook her head, trying to let go of the image of her parents. "Gavin— We saw the car coming. Out of control. If he hadn't pulled me away when he did..." She looked at the bench they'd been sitting on, now a mass of splintered wood. Her stomach roiled. Her heart thundered. "Do you live here?" she asked, confused.

"Above the spa across the street. My sister Dixie's place. What are you doing in town?"

Honeymooning. Becca almost laughed hysterically. She couldn't say that out loud. "We were just—" She stopped. It all seemed so frivolous, when a pregnant woman's life was on the line.

"Do you think she's alive?" Becca asked.

"Gavin's acting like she is."

Another man ran up, carrying a small black bag. "Is that the doctor?"

"Doc Saxon. He's probably Jennifer's doctor. He's the only one in town."

"Dammit," Doc shouted. He dug into his bag, pulled out a blood-pressure cuff and handed it to Gavin, along with a stethoscope. "She was supposed to be at home in bed. She's preeclamptic."

"Why doesn't Gavin get out of the way and let her doctor take over?"

"I don't think Doc would do anything different, do you?"

Sirens pierced the air, the sound getting louder, closer. A fire engine pulled up.

"Gonna need the jaws," someone from the crowd shouted as the three-man crew hopped out.

There was mass movement, hectic and yet efficient, as if choreographed. Everyone knew their job, did their job, and in a very short time, the driver's door was popped open, a backboard brought close and the woman carefully guided onto it in what seemed like super slow motion.

"The ambulance is already on a run," one of the firefighters said. "They've just arrived at the hospital. They can't get here for another thirty, at least."

Gavin pressed the stethoscope to the woman's abdomen. Someone yelled, "Shut up!" Silence descended for a few seconds.

Gavin looked at the doctor and just barely shook his head. "We need to take her ourselves. They won't have a fetal monitor on the ambulance, anyway."

Confusion enveloped Becca like white-hot noise, filling her head like the aftermath of a nuclear explosion, weakening her knees as the truth finally sank in.

"He's a doctor," she said out loud. "A real doctor."

Shana gasped, then swore. "He didn't tell you?"

"He did, in a way, but I thought he was joking.

I thought he was playing the part I'd hired him to do."

"He's an ob-gyn." Shana swore again. "Did you know this was his hometown?"

Becca shook her head. She couldn't talk to Shana about him. She had to think about it, about everything.

"There's only one ambulance?" she asked. "That seems so dangerous."

"One of the disadvantages of rural living. All the firefighters are paramedics, though, so that helps. And then there's Doc, who never takes a vacation."

A large SUV appeared and the woman was loaded in. She came to as the transfer was being made, screaming, begging Doc to save her baby.

"The baby comes first," she yelled over and over.

Becca's throat burned. She didn't know how much distress the baby was in, but from the expressions on Gavin's and the doctor's faces, it didn't look good.

Gavin raced up, digging into his pocket as he got to her and passing her the car keys. "I'll meet you at the cabin later. I know there's a lot that needs saying."

Then he was gone, hopping into the back of the SUV with the doctor. A car pulled up before they could leave, and a young man raced to the SUV and got in. Jennifer's husband probably, in full panic mode. Then the SUV drove away, their cargo precious.

"Do you want to come upstairs with me?" Shana asked. "You look like you're in shock. My little girl is with a friend because I work at the spa on Thursdays."

"No, I can't. I've got Pancho with me. And I kind of have to absorb all this." She gave her a perfunctory hug then headed to the car as if through a tunnel. Pancho barked and wagged his tail, happy to see her. She wanted to curl up next to him, press her face into his fur and hide.

Then anger took over, sweeping through her like a tornado, gathering speed and strength. She was worried about the poor pregnant woman and her baby, but that was out of her hands. What was in her hands was…a mess. She felt like such a fool.

He'd cleared the chaos from her life and now it was back tenfold.

How quickly life could change. Parents could die in an instant on an icy road one winter night. Beliefs could be torn asunder with one lie perpetuated by a man she thought she'd come to love.

She'd done the same thing to people she loved. She'd lied to her brothers. This was payback, swift and cutting.

This was why she never let herself fall in love before. Why she would never love again. For a moment in time, she'd started to believe maybe she'd been wrong, that her life could be different. But now…

She made the drive back to the cabin, packed her

bags and loaded the car. Then she sat in a chair on the front porch, Pancho at her feet, and waited.

Gavin spotted Becca sitting on the porch as he was dropped off hours after the accident. Pancho raced up to him in welcome. Becca stayed in her chair.

"Thanks a lot," he called out to the man who'd brought him home, then he greeted Pancho for a minute before he went to face the music with Becca. But as he walked past her car he saw her suitcase in the backseat. Agonizing shards twisted and turned inside him.

"How is she? How's the baby?" she asked right away.

"Amazingly strong, both of them."

Becca closed her eyes, her shoulders drooped. "Thank God. What did you end up doing?"

"I don't have privileges at that hospital, so I mostly stayed in the lobby. Doc consulted with me some, but she pretty much came through on her own. The air bag and seat belt saved their lives." He sat in the chair beside her. "I saw you talking to Shana."

"Yeah. Funny meeting her here, huh? What a small world."

Becca wasn't usually sarcastic, so it gave him a pretty good idea of how angry she was.

"I was just starting to tell you everything when the car crashed."

"I think that qualifies as too little, too late, Gavin."

He scanned their surroundings, noticed the quiet. Even the birds had stopped singing. Pancho sat between them, facing them, looking from one to the other as they spoke.

"I saw your suitcase in your car. I appreciate your staying until I got back."

"I wanted to know how the woman and baby were."

Ouch. "May I plead my case?"

"I've given that a lot of thought. I decided I wanted to hear your explanation, because I deserve to know the truth. But I'll be leaving right after."

"Fair enough. So. You know I grew up in Chance City, and you know I'm a doctor."

"A little bird told me."

"All I ever wanted was to be a doctor. I believe I'm a good one, but no matter how good we are, statistically doctors will be sued for medical malpractice on the average of about 2.5 times in their career, ob-gyns even more frequently. I guess you also know I really am an ob-gyn."

"The same bird told me."

He nodded. "When I told you I was between jobs, it was because I'd taken a leave from my practice. I'd been sued. It was a very long process, almost a year. I worked until the hearing, during which I was exonerated, but it was as if my world caved in after it was all over. I'd held it together until then. Then I fell apart."

She didn't say anything—made no comment and asked no questions—but she was listening.

"Every time my lawyer questioned me, and then later, my patient's attorney, I searched deep for answers, Becca. They always came back the same. I hadn't done anything wrong. In fact, I saved her life and her baby's. The mother had gone into premature labor, the fetus was in distress. I had to do a C-section. In the end, I also had to do a hysterectomy or she would've bled to death. It was touch and go for the baby for a long time, and now she has major health issues, which in fact were genetic abnormalities, not due to anything I did during surgery."

He stopped, taking a minute to collect his thoughts. "Even shown proof of that, my patient couldn't get past the fact she would never be able to have a second child, and the child she has will probably require care for the rest of her life."

He looked away from the sympathy that had crept into Becca's face. "What most people don't understand is how much anguish we go through any time we're sued. Even when we know we've done no harm, which is our sworn oath."

"Is this the source of your nightmares?"

"How I feel doesn't matter. The end result for that mother and daughter is all that counts. That mother thinks of me every time she looks at her daughter. Nothing will ever be normal for her. It crushes me, her pain."

"Are you returning to your practice?"

He scrubbed his face with his hands. "I've been tormented by doubt for months, but helping that young woman today made me remember how much I love my work, how much it's defined me. It's what I'm trained to do and what I'm good at."

"Is that a roundabout way of saying yes?"

"Yes. I think it'll help me to move on, too, even though I'll never shut it out completely."

"I'm sorry you went through that, Gavin."

"Thank you." He tried to smile. "You probably want to know why I didn't tell you all this."

"I knew you were keeping things from me, and now I feel pretty foolish for questioning you about work. You had a hundred opportunities to tell me. I've been an open book with you. You know I've deceived my brothers and my coworkers. You know all my failures and flaws."

"I see you as a human being, Becca. I know what you perceive are your failures and flaws, but I also know your successes and strengths. I admire you. I fought helping you at first because so much mud was flung at me at the malpractice hearing, so many twists to the truth that I didn't want to be involved in any more lies, period. Ultimately I said yes not only because I felt sympathy for your position, but because I needed to be needed. You gave me purpose."

She hadn't taken her eyes off him, but her expression was indecipherable. He'd gotten to know what she was feeling, based on her expression. Now she'd drawn a curtain.

Her fingers were linked in her lap, her skin gone white.

"You said your first oath as a doctor is to do no harm. Well, as a human being, you harmed, Gavin. You know everything important about me, and I don't know you at all. I feel naive and used," she said, her voice unsteady.

"I humbly apologize. If I could go back, I'd do it differently."

"You know, we wouldn't have worked anyway, Gavin," Becca said with a sigh. "We've never talked about it directly, but you want the things I don't— marriage and children. We let sex blind us."

He didn't have a response to that. They did want different things, but were they really impossible? Minds did change sometimes.

After a moment she stood. Pancho went on alert.

"I have to leave now," she said. "I figure you know enough people who would give you a ride back to Sacramento."

Gavin stood, too. "I wish you wouldn't go."

"I have to figure out a way to tell my brothers and my friends that I lied to them. I don't blame you for that, by the way. That was my doing. And maybe I'm angrier at myself than you. I don't know. But just looking at you reminds me of it. I can't imagine what Eric is going to say. I'm so grateful he flew home yesterday. I need some time."

"I think he may surprise you. He really hadn't

understood how much he's smothered you." *In his effort to try to save you from yourself, Becca.* But that was for her and Eric to come to terms with.

"Yeah, well, apparently I've needed smothering, which didn't help, after all, either. But here's my point. I never lied to *you*. Everything I said and did was real. You can't say the same. Goodbye, Gavin." She went down the stairs. Pancho followed her. She stopped, looked at him, then at Gavin. "The marriage may be over, but it looks like we've got a custody issue here."

"Take him." He figured she needed him more. Pancho was a symbol of something for her. Gavin wasn't sure what yet. "I'll go get his things."

But just then Pancho looked at Gavin and took a couple of steps toward him.

"What now?" she asked. "Neither one of us has any right to keep him, you know. He deserves better than a workaholic owner."

"I don't intend to be that person anymore. And I'm optimistic that you won't be, either. I hope it's the lesson we take from all this, Becca. A hard, but good lesson."

She studied his face for a few seconds, then went on to her car. She opened the back door. Pancho made a move toward her then slowed. Then he sat. She started to get in her car then went back to the dog and hugged him.

"Goodbye, pooch. Have a good life."

Gavin thought she was talking to *him* as much as to the dog.

"Same to you," he whispered as she drove off.

Pancho met him on the porch, looking sad, not accusatory, as Gavin might have thought. Poor dog. He'd lost his owner, and now his friend.

"Looks like it's you and me. Is that okay with you?"

Pancho barked, and they headed into the house. The empty house that just this morning was teeming with laughter and sweet lovemaking.

He didn't think he could stay there without her, so he pulled out his phone and called the one person he could talk to, then waited to be picked up.

In the meantime he started creating a plan. A life plan. Starting here, starting now.

Chapter Fifteen

Her loft was too perfect, Becca decided as she burrowed into her sofa wrapped in her fleecy robe, her feet on the coffee table, alternately digging crackers out of a box and sipping Chardonnay. All the healthy food had gone to the cabin with them or been eaten by Eric, and she hadn't gone shopping yet. It'd only been three days since she'd walked away from Gavin. She hadn't been able to rouse herself enough to leave her home, had lived on what little was left in her cupboards, supplemented with pizza delivery.

She was sick of pizza.

Tomorrow she would have to go back to work. Until then she planned to continue to wallow.

The television had been on since she'd walked in

the door Thursday afternoon. She'd watched mostly
old movies that made her cry, even the comedies.
She hadn't slept in her bed, in fact, couldn't. She'd
stripped the sheets and washed them but hadn't put
them back on. She'd turned her living room into her
sanctuary.

Their wedding bands lay on the coffee table, small,
circular neon reminders of what could have been.
He'd put them in her suitcase in case they'd needed
them during the trip but hadn't worn them. She had
to get them back to him.

Of course there was the small matter to consider
of not having his address. She'd fallen in love with
him, made love with him, had given him her trust
and didn't even know where he lived.

If that wasn't a sign of how blind she'd been…
Blind and stupid.

She missed Pancho, too. His unconditional love.
The trust that had grown between them.

She hadn't called Eric yet, was debating about
flying to New York to speak with him in person. She
didn't want to tell anyone at work until Eric knew, so
she had to seem honeymoon happy tomorrow, even
with Suki. Becca had done enough pretending. Facing
more of it seemed too daunting.

Her cell phone rang. She looked at the caller ID,
saw it was Eric, ordered herself to buck up and said
hello.

"I was hoping I'd catch you," he said. "Are

you home? On the road? At the cabin still? How was it?"

"Home. The cabin was fabulous, Eric. A gem. And the countryside was spectacular. Thank you again. It was a generous gift." She closed her eyes, prepared herself to tell him—

"I'm coming to Sacramento on Wednesday," he said. "I'll be house hunting."

Becca's throat closed. She'd gotten another reprieve. She would wait to tell him in person, take the lecture she was sure he would give her like the adult she'd been trying to convince him she was. He'd never believe that now.

"That's great," she managed to say. "You can stay here."

"Thanks for the offer, but I won't intrude on you newlyweds."

"Gavin…Gavin won't be here. Please stay with me, Eric."

"If you insist."

"I do."

"Are you okay?" he asked. "You sound, I don't know, stressed?"

"I'm good. Everything's okay." Yet another lie. "I can't wait to see you." Which was the truth. Or at least until she had to face him.

They talked a little longer, then within seconds after they hung up, her phone rang again. She answered it without looking at the ID, figuring Eric had forgotten something.

"Hi, Becca." It was Gavin. "I'm sorry to bother you," he said when she didn't speak. She didn't know what to say.

"It's fine."

"Good. Um, I need to return the rings to the jeweler."

"I have them." *I've been staring at them for days. They've been my touchstone for staying mad at you.*

"Can I come up? I'm in your parking garage picking up my car."

"Did you stay at the cabin until now?" How could he? It was their honeymoon place, their love nest, their—

"I stayed in Chance City, yes. Can I come up?" he repeated.

There was no way she was going to let him see her wallowing, her hair a mess, unshowered, wearing her old bathrobe. "I'll put them outside my door for you."

"Becca—"

"I don't want to see you, Gavin." *I hurt too much.*

"Or Pancho?"

"You're keeping him for sure?"

"He's pretty much glued himself to me. I've... needed him, too. To get by. I miss you, Becca."

Crap. Tears welled, hot and burning. "I'm putting the rings outside right now." She hung up, not even saying goodbye, because she couldn't get the word out. She'd already done that once.

Becca scooped up the rings, opened her front door and set them outside. She held vigil at the peephole, making sure no one else came along. After a minute he approached, Pancho trotting next to him. He paused at the door, stooped down, then stood. He didn't walk away. He set his hand against the door, waiting. He could've spoken and she would've heard him, but he didn't.

Finally, he walked away, saying, "Come on, boy."

And Becca turned her back to the door, crumpled to the ground and cried.

How could she still love him after what he'd done?

He was in pain, Becca. He told you the agony he'd been through. Have a heart.

I do have a heart, and it's broken.

Imagine how he feels. He pretty much told you he felt the same.

Without stopping to debate, she pulled open the door but he was already gone. She couldn't go after him like this.

Fate, she decided. It wasn't meant to be.

Time to move on.

Chip called a meeting of the cofounders first thing Monday morning. Everyone wondered aloud what was going on. They usually met midafternoon. Becca was glad. There hadn't been time to be teased about her honeymoon, hadn't had to evade. She would tell them after she'd told Eric. Period.

Chip strode in and took his place at the head of the table. "Good morning, everyone. I've got news. Crandall Computing has made an offer to buy us out."

He let everyone react before continuing. Becca kept her eyes on Chip, trying to gauge how he felt about it. He wasn't an openly emotional man, so it was hard to judge.

"Only the six of us have votes in this decision." He wrote a huge number with lots of zeroes on the whiteboard next to him. "Here's the offer. On top of that, we're all guaranteed jobs, although probably not the same ones for everyone. I'd be going in as a VP. Becca, your position would change, too, since they already have a VP of operations, but your negotiating experience is something they're keen on."

She could barely take it all in. She was already running on empty. Then to add this to it—

"As you probably know," Chip went on, "Crandall's located in the Silicon Valley. Corporate headquarters is in Palo Alto. Obviously it's going to require a move, since it's about ninety miles from here. Becca, I know you just bought your place, and you'll probably factor that in. The rest of us haven't gotten around to buying, so the move's easier in that sense. Initial reactions, everyone?"

"Is that deal a six-way split?" Morgan asked.

"Almost. If any of our employees wants to make the move, I'd like to help them do that. It's expensive. There will be closing costs here. So, probably about a seven-way split. It's still a helluva lot of money."

"I'm game," Jacob said. "Closer to San Francisco. It's, what, about thirty miles or so?"

"How did this deal happen?" Becca asked, finding her voice. Thirty miles to San Francisco, instead of eighty from Sacramento? Would it make a difference? Could she and Gavin—

She couldn't think about that. She had to make decisions based on what was good for her, only her.

"Greg Crandall called me yesterday at home. I didn't approach him, if that's what you're asking. You know what the company is worth now, and it's because we've put a lot of hard work into it. We're being rewarded. We lived on little for a long time to get to this point."

"Is this something you want to do?" Becca asked.

"Yes. But I welcome any and all debate. I'm sure you'll think of reasons why or why not that I haven't."

Fifteen minutes later they unanimously agreed to the deal. They may not own their own business anymore, but they had the financial security to make their own choices—the American dream come true for six thirty-year-olds who'd started with an innovative idea then made it happen.

"Let's go get breakfast," Becca said to Suki as

they left the conference room. "I'm too keyed up to work."

The café was only a block away. It felt good to be outdoors in the beautiful May morning.

"Unbelievable, huh?" Suki said after they'd been served coffee and placed their orders. Becca missed Gavin fixing her breakfast, making her eat and take a moment before she rushed to work.

She missed Gavin, period.

"Unbelievable," Becca agreed.

"We're rich, Bec."

"If we're careful with it. Are you going to move? Take a job there?"

"Absolutely. How about you?"

Becca sipped her coffee as she considered her answer. "I want to know more about the job. And, you know, I just got my loft looking good. Plus Eric's decided to move to Sacramento. I'd like to have family close by for a change. It's a big decision." One she wouldn't rush to make.

"So what happened with Gavin, can I ask? You've been so quiet. Did you really go away with him last week?"

"Yes. I fell for him, Suki. Hard." It felt surprisingly good to say it out loud. "Get this. He really is a doctor."

Suki gasped then laughed, and the mood lightened considerably.

"You never looked him up on Google, Becca? You?"

"I know. Crazy, huh?"

They lingered over breakfast, enjoying their first time alone in a couple of weeks before they returned to the office, where the news wouldn't be shared with the staffers until the deal was done.

The next day, Tuesday, the six partners drove to Palo Alto to discuss job particulars. The ride back to Sacramento was surprisingly quiet as each of them mulled over their own decisions of whether to move or not. They'd promised the people at Crandall they'd have answers by the end of the week. In the meantime, there was still work to be done and they did it.

Then Wednesday Becca left work early, at five-thirty. Eric was supposed to arrive by seven, and she needed to clean up the house. She took the elevator up, turned the corner of her hallway and saw him sitting on the floor by her door, waiting.

"Why didn't you call?" she asked.

It wasn't Eric but Gavin. Waiting. Just like when they first met.

Then a dog came charging at her. Pancho jumped up on her and danced around her on his hind legs. Becca took a minute to greet him, to steady herself.

Gavin stood. "Hi."

"Hi." He looked good. Great, in fact. Rested.

"I didn't call because I wasn't sure you would see me, and I really needed to see you."

"I thought you were Eric," she said, putting her

key in the door, feeling him near her. She'd missed him so much. So very much. "He's supposed to be here tonight. He's coming to house hunt."

Pancho ran past both of them and went on the hunt, sniffing everything, checking out every room in record time then returning to be petted. He seemed to be grinning, which made her laugh.

"Thank you for letting me in," Gavin said. "There are some things that I need to say."

"Me, too." They sat on the couch at opposite ends. Pancho curled up under her coffee table. "Can I go first?"

"Sure."

"I've given your…situation a lot of thought, Gavin. In fact, I've thought of little else, and believe me, there's been plenty else I should've been making decisions about. Instead I've been in full avoidance mode. I got it finally. I understand why you kept things from me. Maybe not that you kept me in the dark for the whole time, but certainly at the beginning. I think you should've trusted me by the time we got to the cabin, but I keep trying to look at it through your eyes."

"Believe me, I can see it from your side, Becca."

She finally noticed he'd gotten his hair cut, although not too much. Because she liked it longer?

"You look really good, Gavin. You've always been pretty calm, but this is different. This is something else. You seem at peace."

He smiled. "I've been having flying dreams."

"I take it that's a good thing."

"Yes."

Her heart warmed at his words, at his obvious peace. She reached over and touched his hand. Just like the first time, electricity sizzled between them. She pulled back reluctantly.

"What's changed for you?" she asked.

"I've accepted a new job. I'm going to replace Doc Saxon in Chance City."

Nothing could've surprised her more. Nothing. Just when she'd thought she was moving to Palo Alto to be geographically closer to him. "What brought that on?"

"Doc's seventy-three. He's been wanting to retire for a couple of years, but he couldn't find a replacement. A lot of people have been pushing me to take over, but I always laughed. I had a practice in San Francisco. I loved the city life. My parents were in Chance City, and they were part of the reason I left."

"So, what's different?"

"Me. Because of you."

Her heart began to pound. He slid closer to her. "In trying to help you find a slower pace, to enjoy life more, I found it for myself. I don't want that hectic life anymore, with the long hours and little time for fun."

He hadn't said the words yet that she wanted to hear. "How do you make a move like that? You're an ob-gyn. You would be a rural family doctor."

"Because I'm an overachiever, I did a double residency. I knew I'd end up being a primary-care doctor for a lot of my patients. I wanted to know it all."

"Of course you did." She smiled at the thought. He really was a fascinating man.

"The job comes with a house—the one Doc lived in with his late wife and children. It needs an overhaul, which Kincaid will start on next week. The compensation will be a far cry from what I'm used to. I had a long talk with Doc right after you left, and he was completely honest about what I should expect, including bartering for food sometimes as payment, but he says it keeps his freezer full."

He looked so happy. She wanted to be that happy, too. But she was afraid to be.

"I'm in love with you, Becca. I'm pretty sure it was love at first sight, or I wouldn't have agreed to your wild scheme."

"Gavin—"

"Wait, please. I'm not done. I need to tell you I figured it out."

She frowned. "Figured what— Oh. The night I told you I was never going to marry or have children."

"You wouldn't tell me why. You just told me to figure it out. I did. It all started with the dog figurines. They reminded you of your parents, didn't they? Were they gifts?"

"Yes." She forced the word out. "Birthdays, Christmas, Easter. Whenever."

"Because you couldn't have a dog. Because of Jeff's allergies."

She nodded, looked at her lap.

He put a finger under her chin, raising it. "But that isn't everything, is it? That's not what you wanted me to figure out."

She shook her head.

He finally took her hands in his. "You're afraid to love. Afraid you might die young and leave your children without their mother."

"It's too hard, Gavin." Her voice cracked. "Being an orphan. I can't take that chance of leaving my children that way."

"I can't imagine how you feel. I can only tell you again that I love you. That I want you, need you in my life forever. I think you love me, too. Take a chance, Becca. There are no guarantees in life, only the hope of a long life and happiness. Do you think you'll be happy without love?"

Pancho maneuvered himself to put his head in her lap.

"See? He's asking you, too. He needs you, too. Take a chance. Be ours."

She bent over Pancho and kissed his head, and then she smiled at Gavin, everything becoming crystal clear. "I love you, too."

He closed his eyes for several seconds, holding his breath, then let it out in a long stream. And then he kissed her, not a soft meeting of lips but hard and desperate, putting all his emotions into it. They clung to each other, aware of how differently it could've turned out if… Just *if.*

"I have to live in Chance City, Becca. There's no way around that. I know it would be a long commute for you, and you work such long hours, too, but I hope it'll be worth it. I love you. I want to marry you and have children with you. In Chance City, the best place I can think of to do that."

There was so much to tell him. She wouldn't make the move with the company. She would find something new and challenging to do, with the man she loved by her side. Eric would live an hour away. Life would be so sweet.

The doorbell rang. Eric was early. She flung open the door, happiness rushing through her. She had a lot of explaining to do, but Gavin would be there with her, too.

"So, big brother," she said, excited and teary eyed. "How would you like to walk me down the aisle?"

* * * * *

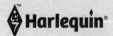
Harlequin®

COMING NEXT MONTH
Available May 31, 2011

SPECIAL EDITION

HSECNM0511

REQUEST YOUR FREE BOOKS!

2 FREE NOVELS PLUS 2 FREE GIFTS!

◆ Harlequin®

SPECIAL EDITION

Life, Love & Family

Harlequin® Blaze™ brings you
New York Times *and* USA TODAY *bestselling author*
Vicki Lewis Thompson with three new steamy titles
from the bestselling miniseries SONS OF CHANCE

Chance isn't just the last name of these rugged
Wyoming cowboys—it's their motto, too!

Read on for a sneak peek at the first title,
SHOULD'VE BEEN A COWBOY

Available June 2011 only from Harlequin® Blaze™.

"THANKS FOR NOT TURNING ON THE LIGHTS," Tyler said. "I'm a mess."

"Not in my book." Even in low light, Alex had a good view of her yellow shirt plastered to her body. It was all he could do not to reach for her, mud and all. But the next move needed to be hers, not his.

She slicked her wet hair back and squeezed some water out of the ends as she glanced upward. "I like the sound of the rain on a tin roof."

"Me, too."

She met his gaze briefly and looked away. "Where's the sink?"

"At the far end, beyond the last stall."

Tyler's running shoes squished as she walked down the aisle between the rows of stalls. She glanced sideways at Alex. "So how much of a cowboy are you these days? Do you ride the range and stuff?"

"I ride." He liked being able to say that. "Why?"

"Just wondered. Last summer, you were still a city boy. You even told me you weren't the cowboy type, but you're…different now."

He wasn't sure if that was a good thing or a bad thing. Maybe she preferred city boys to cowboys. "How am I different?"

"Well, you dress differently, and your hair's a little longer. Your face seems a little more chiseled, but maybe that's because of your hair. Also, there's something else, something harder to define, an attitude…"

"Are you saying I have an attitude?"

"Not in a bad way. It's more like a quiet confidence."

He was flattered, but still he had to laugh. "I just admitted a while ago that I have all kinds of doubts about this event tomorrow. That doesn't seem like quiet confidence to me."

"This isn't about your job, it's about…your…" She took a deep breath. "It's about your sex appeal, okay? I have no business talking about it, because it will only make me want to do things I shouldn't do." She started toward the end of the barn. "Now, where's that sink? We need to get cleaned up and go back to the house. Dinner is probably ready, and I—"

He spun her around and pulled her into his arms, mud and all. "Let's do those things." Then he kissed her, knowing that she would kiss him back, knowing that this time he would take that kiss where he wanted it to go. And she would let him.

Follow Tyler and Alex's wild adventures in
SHOULD'VE BEEN A COWBOY
Available June 2011 only from Harlequin® Blaze™
wherever books are sold.

SPECIAL EDITION

Life, Love and Family

LOVE CAN BE FOUND IN THE MOST UNLIKELY PLACES, ESPECIALLY WHEN YOU'RE NOT LOOKING FOR IT...

Failed marriages, broken families and disappointment. Cecilia and Brandon have both been unlucky in love and life and are ripe for an intervention. Good thing Brandon's mother happens to stumble upon this matchmaking project. But will Brandon be able to open his eyes and get away from his busy career to see that all he needs is right there in front of him?

FIND OUT IN
WHAT THE SINGLE DAD WANTS...

BY *USA TODAY* BESTSELLING AUTHOR
MARIE FERRARELLA

AVAILABLE IN JUNE 2011
WHEREVER BOOKS ARE SOLD.

www.eHarlequin.com

SE0611MF